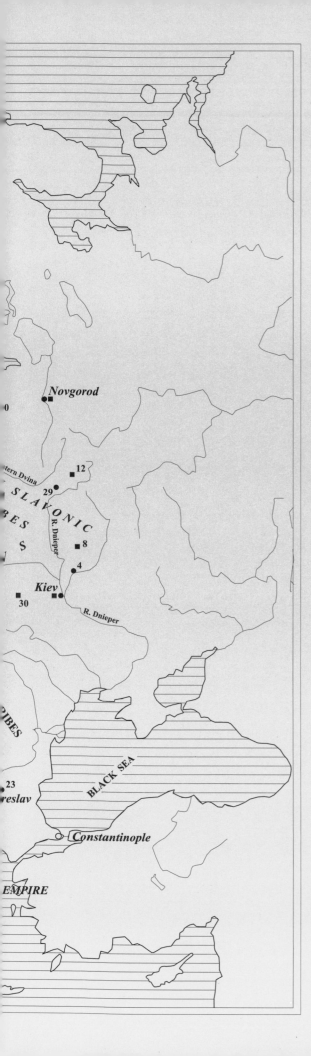

LEGEND

● CULT FIGURINES AND PAGAN GODS

■ PAGAN CULT SITES - SANCTUARIES

▲ PAGAN SANCTUARIES WITH TEMPLES

✝ BISHOPRIC - ARCHBISHOPRIC

┋ GREAT MORAVIA
(Moravians - Slovenes (Slovaks))

1	●	Altfriesack
2	●	Bresalauspurc (Bratislava)
3	●	Dowina (Devín)
4	●	Chernigov
5	▲	Feldberg
6	▲	Gross Raden (Schwerin)
7	●■	Halich - Bogit
8	■	Khodovisichi (near the lake Svjatoe)
9	●	Jankow
10	●	Jarovka
11	●■	Kiev
12	■	Krasnogorskoje
13	●	Merseburg
14	■	Michajlovgrad - Montana
15	✝●■	Mikulčice
16	■▲	Neubrandeburg
17	✝	Nitrava
18	●■	Novgorod
19	■	Oldenburg - Stargrad (Wagria)
20	●	Opole
21	■	Pohansko
22	✝●■	Praha
23	●	Preslav
24	■▲	Rethra
25	■▲	Rostock
26	■▲	Rugen - Arkona, Garz, Ralswieck
27	●■	Stará Kouřim
28	■▲	Stettin
29	■	Tushemlja
30	■	Shumsk
31	●	Wiślica
32	■▲	Wolin

Tales from
Slavic Myths

Tales from
Slavic Myths

Ivan Hudec

Translation by Emma Nezinska & Jeff Schmitz
with Albert Devine
Afterword by Dusan Caplovic
Illustrated by Karol Ondreicka

Bolchazy-Carducci
Publishers, Inc.
Wauconda, Illinois

This book has received a subsidy from
The National Centre
for Slovak Literature in Bratislava
&
The Slovak-American
International Cultural Foundation, Inc.

Translators
Emma Nezinska and Jeff Schmitz with Albert Devine
Copyfitting and Typography
Charlene M. Hernandez

Published by
Bolchazy-Carducci Publishers, Inc.
1000 Brown Street, #101
Wauconda, Illinois 60084 USA
http://www.bolchazy.com

ISBN: 0-86516-451-7

Printed in Slovakia
2001
by Vydavateľstvo Ofprint

Library of Congress Cataloging-in-Publication Data

Hudec, Ivan, 1947-
[Báje a mýty starých Slovanov. English]
Tales from slavic myths / Ivan Hudec ; translation by Emma Nezinska & Jeff Schmitz ; afterword by Dusan Caplovic ; illustrated by Karol Ondreicka
p. cm.
ISBN 0-86516-451-7
1. Mythology, Slavic. 2. Gods, Slavic. 3. Slavs—religion. I. Title.

BL930 .H83 2000
299'.18—dc21

00-039792

CHAPTER 1
The Age of Dreams

TABLE OF CONTENTS

SVAROG
the Father of the Gods

Svarog is the most ancient of the gods and the creator of the Universe. To him the entire expanse of time given to mankind is but one night of sleep. He spends this night curled up like a baby inside the orb of the Sun, gathering strength to begin his labors again. The Sun is a great egg, glowing golden and blinding to all but the other gods.

As Svarog sleeps, his hands are folded in his lap and his palms feel the spot where his third leg is slowly growing. His nine heads rest wearily on his knees. The entire time of an Era is merely one night to Svarog and he takes no notice of it. His divine day, Sweeping Day, when he begins each new Era, is similarly unremarkable to him.

While Svarog sleeps, a warmth and light emanate from his mighty chest that is powerful enough to maintain peace and order in the Universe. When Svarog's godly night is coming to an end, the light he sends out grows weaker. Finally Svarog's light reaches a point when it is too weak and there is nothing left that is strong enough to keep the huge Universe at peace. A time of formless Chaos then takes its turn, and disorder and discord reign. This time is short-lived, and it is accompanied by a deafening rumble and deep rolling thunder throughout the bleak darkness that engulfs everything. Thick, foul clouds of smoke and dust are stirred up and sent swirling around the Universe.

The incredible tumult awakens Svarog. The heat is gone even from the Sun and the piercing cold makes Svarog shivery, so he sneezes. Then, anxious, he feels for his third leg, making sure the damaged limb has been completely restored. Finding it whole, Svarog is relieved and able to get to work. He stretches his long arms, reaching wider and wider, until he cannot even see his hands anymore. Now he is ready to clean up the mess that has been the Universe. The Father of the Gods heaps everything together, from icy saw-toothed debris to dust and mud and ashes, and even the soot and fumes. Nothing, no matter how tiny, escapes Svarog's divine reach on Sweeping Day as he collects the fragments of the shattered Universe together. At this point only Svarog and the dismembered pieces of the Universe exist.

This is when Svarog's task is the most difficult. Rolling up his sleeves, he takes the huge pile of wreckage and begins kneading the sweepings with his powerful hands. Even Chaos is painstakingly and neatly kneaded into the pile with all the other sweepings. Svarog moans and groans at his labor as his hands, moving in wild circular motions, turn red-hot. Still he toils, panting, his enormous body twisting and convulsing while his heaving chest begins to give off a fierce glow. Svarog, though, doesn't notice or care about anything but the work of kneading the pile. Savagely he kneads and kneads, making the pile smaller and smaller. After a long time the pile is no larger than a boulder, the size of his ninth head, and yet he continues. When the pile has become as small as his fist, Svarog takes the lump in his hands to continue kneading even more vigorously. Rolling between his palms, the mass gradually becomes a ball the size of a tiny pea.

The tiny ball gets smaller and smaller, yet Svarog, choking from his labors, continues kneading diligently until it is no larger than a crumb. Now Svarog finally stops kneading and takes a deep breath. With a horrifying roar he smashes the tiny crumb ferociously against his third leg. Svarog bellows again from the unbearable pain as his third leg shatters and falls off. The enormous energy packed into the tiny crumb from the kneading is released in a violent explosion from the force of the impact and spreads wide in all directions. The Father of the Gods then lets out a third roar, this time as much in triumph as in pain.

From the largest piece of Svarog's shattered third leg sprouts his son, Svarozhich. Jaded with pain, Svarog explains quickly to his son what remains to be done. Then, nearing exhaustion, Svarog picks the most wondrous of the many balls of light that were scattered throughout the Universe by the explosion and makes this a bed for himself. This is when Svarog's Sweeping Day labors are finally at an end and he can afford to fall asleep for his one thousand times one thousand year repose, until he is awakened anew at the close of this Era by the invincible Chaos.

SVAROG—the chief god of the Early Slavs, presides over beginnings and is the patron of "celestial fire". Accounts of Svarog have commonly identified him with his Greek counterpart, the lame god and divine smith Hephaestus. Svarog, the personification of the sky, light and warmth (fire), was conceived of as the creator of all things as well as the law-giver. He was thought of as being the Father of the Gods, who ranked among the principal deities of the older generation. Once the world was created, the role of Svarog as the demiurge waned and the most ancient of the Slavic gods appears to have withdrawn from outer activity, to remain concealed in the background, his cult gradually falling into oblivion and losing out to new rites and rituals. Tradition asserts that in his role as a legislator he had established a range of laws and customs, including a monogamy law binding for both men and women. Offenders, the law decreed, would have to be flung into a fiery furnace. Some myths claim that Svarog, a dextrous artisan, dropped his blacksmith's tongs from the sky. Thenceforth people have been crafting arms and armor to hunt animals and wage wars.

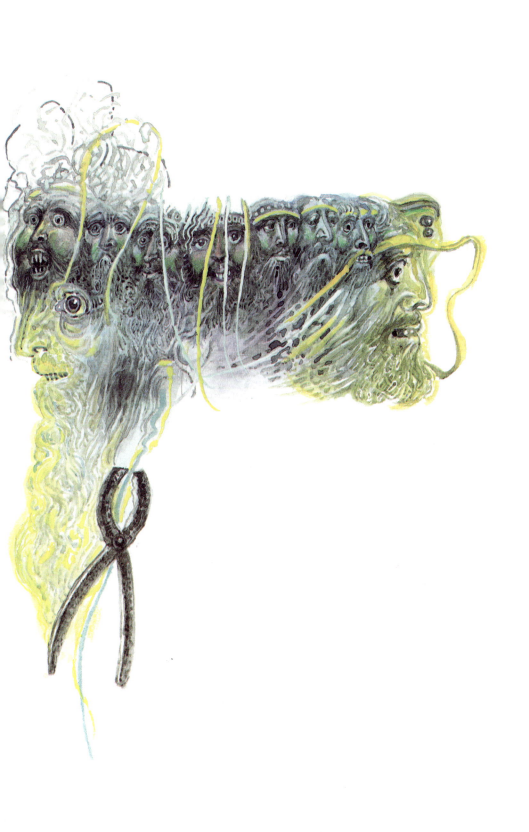

SVAROZHICH
the Supreme Deity of the Slavs

S varozhich, the sun god, the god of the homestead fire and the chief god of this Era, understood perfectly what he was to do. Carefully, he helped his exhausted father, Svarog, into his hot bed inside the Sun. Svarozhich had barely laid his father's legs in the bed when Svarog fell asleep. If the gods allowed any mortal to look straight into the Sun without being struck blind, the beholder could see Svarog as he sleeps, nestled warmly in his bed. Svarozhich then gathered up the smaller pieces of Svarog's shattered third leg and laid them near the Sun, where Svarog's warmth allowed them to grow into the other, lesser gods. Of all the gods and goddesses, only Pizamar, the goddess of music and art, was not created from the remains of Svarog's third leg.

As soon as he was done with this, Svarozhich headed straight for the middle of the stardust, to the innermost part of the explosion, at breakneck speed. There, in a cloud of white-yellow dust that tasted of milk and honey, grazed a horse with a golden mane. Guarding the horse was a golden rooster, keeping a constant vigil by allowing one eye to sleep while the other kept watch. The cunning Svarozhich devised a plan to slip past the rooster on the side that was asleep. Softly he crept up on the golden-maned stallion, using his many eyes to make sure that the rooster's eye was still shut while also watching the nostrils of the horse. If the horse had seen Svarozhich it would have begun neighing, which would have awakened the rooster. The bird would then have started to crow loudly, scaring off the horse. If the events had unfolded like that, Svarozhich would never have caught the quick-footed

ANIMAL-WORSHIP AND SLAVIC PAGAN CULTS—The pagan imagination of the Early Slavs, which endowed natural phenomena with the qualities of life and thought, attached much importance to the creatures of the animal world, placing them upon a higher level. In observing their many cults as well as practising rites and customs, Early Slavs employed statuary representing gods (idols) in human form as well as clay animal likenesses. That animal offerings were common is supported by records and extensive archeological finds.

In Mikulcice, Moravia, a cult site has been unearthed. It featured coarsely-molded clay representations of animals and birds dating back to the pre-Great Moravian period. One example is a statuette of a wild boar from the cult center of Rethra. Another prominent find is that of European bison skulls

13

stallion and the state of the world would have been in jeopardy. But Svarozhich, with many eyes on all sides of his head, was incapable of making a mistake. He quickly captured the golden-maned stallion, haltered it, and leapt on its back.

Having captured and tamed the celestial horse Svarozhich rode back to the Sun. The other gods were there waiting for him, and one, Dazhbog, had already created a beautiful chariot. Svarozhich harnessed the horse to the chariot and rolled the Sun-egg inside. Then, holding the reins tightly, he drew the Sun-egg up to the top of the heavens. From the very first day of our Era onward Svarozhich has driven his chariot across the skies, surveying every corner of the world. On this daily journey Svarozhich is extremely careful to let nothing disturb the sleep of his father, Svarog.

unearthed in Nakla, Poland, providing evidence of a mass animal sacrifice for auspices.

Among the Slavs, a fertility spirit appears to have been typified by the serpent, one of the most potent Slavic symbols. The horse, like the wild boar and horned cattle, was venerated. In Brandenburg, Pomerania, and on the territory populated by the Eastern Slavs, there have been discovered all kinds of tiny statuettes representing horses, some saddled. The horse image was frequently molded in necklace pendants. It was, in all likelihood, represented as the principal attendant of war gods. These quadrupeds also served important functions in the practice of auspices as the means of foretelling the outcome of wars and battles.

Dogs, often encountered in tombs and sepulchral mounds, were looked upon by the heathen as the symbol of faithfulness. Likewise cocks, associated with the break of the dawn, as well as hens, chickens, and eggs, appear to have attained significance in the eyes of Early Slavs and were commonly placed in graves. This ancient Slavic custom was perpetuated well into the Middle Ages, even following the adoption of Christianity. Painted clay eggs, referred to as pisanky, and decorated with solar and fertility patterns, were widely spread among most groups of the Early Slavs. The accuracy of the tradition has often been confirmed. Such eggs

The world that Svarozhich rode over was vast and knew no bounds. To avoid confusion among the many lesser gods that he ruled over, Svarozhich named the four points of the compass. Ever since then they have been known as the midnight quarter, or north, the midday quarter, or south, the morning quarter, or east, and the evening side, or west.

After these regions were assigned names, Svarozhich appointed the strongest and wisest among the other gods to rule over these areas. This group of divine kings was Radhost, or Radegast, Dazhbog, Svantovit, and Perun. Once these gods assumed command of the world's regions, Svarozhich was able to begin the task of creating Time.

It may seem that Time should have been created earlier than after the division of the world, but until then there was simply no need for it. Svarog, the Father of the Gods, has no need of Time since he is immortal. But Svarozhich, who was begotten of his father's limb, is mortal in the eyes of Svarog, since Svarozhich will only reign until the end of this Era. This made Svarozhich very aware of Time. He felt compelled to create and compute Time for guidance and order.

Time is very important to Svarozhich for imposing order on the Universe. He must arrange events one after another and not allow them to stumble onto each other, occur alongside each other, or take place all at once. With Time to guide him, Svarozhich keeps events in their proper order, one after another. Svarozhich also imposed the necessity of events to flow from other events, a situation that people came to understand in terms of cause and effect. Everything follows a certain progression and Time requires patience for things to complete their cycle. For example, a seed cannot be planted and harvested at the same moment.

Following the creation of Time, Svarozhich merged it with the four quarters of the world to create Motion. Motion helps produce fire, makes earth and water move, and assists Svarozhich in the creation of all other things.

have been discovered in Poland and, quite recently, in Slovakia, during archeological excavations carried out in Nitra-Drazovce and Bratislava. The name survives in contemporary Ukrainian as the term for an Easter egg, pysanka.

When he had finished with these things, Svarozhich felt very content. However, he was prudent as well, and decided not to simply leave things to themselves. So he created Fate and assigned it the task of spinning the thread of human destiny. Fate, however, may be obscure, as well as injurious and grudging. It is fortunate, then, that those with great craft and cunning have a chance to cheat or outwit the deity that controls human destiny.

To ensure his control over such a vast world Svarozhich then created and appointed aides, known as demons, to manage the world's smaller regions. There are many demons as there is much that they must attend to, such as fire, earth, water, and air. Later Svarozhich would give assignments to the other gods, deciding which ones would rule over which of the primordial demons.

What the
CHIEF GODS
Look Like

Svarozhich, the su-preme god, has a head like a ball that has many eyes, mouths, and ears all around it and is constantly spinning. This is so that the divine head may, at once, see and hear everything that is happening in the world, as well as speak in all corners of the world. The head spins unevenly, changing speeds and directions at will.

Svarozhich's golden-maned horse is harnessed to a magnificent chariot that is used to draw the Sun across the sky. Every morning, holding tightly to the reins, Svarozhich sets off in the chariot. Many people try to catch a glimpse of Svarozhich in his chariot by waiting all night on high mountains, but all they can ever see is the glimmer of the morning light. The brightness of the Sun would blind humans if they were to look directly at it, and the light reflecting off the chariot is equally bright, making it impossible to ever see Svarozhich.

Perun is the quick-tempered and much-dreaded storm god, whose roar makes the thunder boom and who hurls lightning bolts down at the world. The infinite danger of his wrath is offset by an equally infinite blessing. When enraged, Perun causes thunderstorms and sends his forked lightning to split the skies, which causes the heavens to break into tears, bringing rain to the earth. The rains fertilize the thirsty ground, fostering the fruits of the earth, which then yields richer harvests. This is why Perun is not only the god of thunder and lightning, but also the god of the harvest. Perun resides in a dreary, dank, and remote corner of his realm in the midnight region of the earth. No one has ever managed to describe

his ferocious face, because mortals would be overcome with fear and die if they were to gaze on it. Even when Perun does not strike with his thunderbolts, he can cause great destruction by stamping his foot so hard that the earth breaks open and swallows everything in the area. Yet the malevolent Perun can be placated fairly easily. He enjoys sacrificial offerings, particularly when huge tongues of flame devour old oak which Perun himself likes to set on fire with his bolts of lightning. The sight of a tree ablaze makes the god feel good, for it is this fire that feeds his strength.

Radhost, or Radegast, rules over the evening quarter of the world and lives far in the west. Raven-haired, with deep-set black eyes that glow like embers in his black face, Radhost is the god of fire, and rules the fires of the twilight and night stars. He is also known as the guardian of the night lights of the world's wanderers. Svarozhich created Radhost almost in his own image, except for giving Radhost only one set of eyes and ears, and only one mouth. At the spring and autumn equinox, the times when the sun and the shadow meet, sacrificial offerings are made to Radhost. The winter and summer solstices, known as Krachun, and Bathing Festival, Christianized as St. John the Baptist Day, are also important times for feasting in honor of Radhost.

The realm of Svantovit is the midday side of the world. Svantovit is illustrious, and known as the favorite of Svarozhich, enjoying more privileges than the other gods. Svarozhich regards Svantovit so highly that he gave Svantovit four vigilant heads so that he may see in all directions at once. This ability allows Svantovit the special honor of filling in for Svarozhich when Svarozhich is unavailable.

Dazhbog is a youthful, radiant god whose beauty often arouses the jealousy of the goddesses as they vie for his attention. Seemingly cold, Dazhbog hides a passionate heart, one that is able to light up and start days, and dawn is merely the embers fanned by Dazhbog. After the cold nights, Svarozhich warms up his stiff hands over the light of Dazhbog's heart before he draws the Sun up into the

CHERNOBOG (Chiernoglav), the Black God—The functions of this deity appear to have overlapped with Radhost's. Chernobog seems to have been regarded with great veneration as the god of war and victory, particularly across Slavic countries of the Baltic region. Some of those territories are in present-day Poland and Germany.

SVANTOVIT—He is the Slavic god of war and pre-server of the fields. He was esteemed as one of the prin-cipal deities of the Western Slavs. Svantovit is referred to in the chronicles of the twelfth century when his cult must have reached its zenith. This deity displayed attributes expected of a war god and patron of husbandry. His horn filled with wine was used by Slavic priests in the divination for the harvest of the forthcoming year. A large honey cake was used for similar purposes. Among Svantovit's war insignia are a sword, a spear, and the sacred horse called 'Belush' (which translates as something like 'whitish horse'). Only a priest and Svantovit him-self were allowed to ride this horse.

sky. Svarozhich's golden-maned horse is kept in a stable on Dazhbog's morning side. Radhost, Svantovit, and Perun frown disapprovingly when they see people worshipping Svarozhich in the morning because they know that in doing so those people also honor Dazhbog. So the three gods take pleasure in playing mean tricks on Dazhbog, mainly by bringing gloomy weather to hide the sunrise behind clouds.

How
OUR WORLD
Was Created

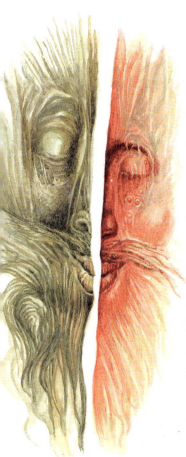

Before falling asleep inside the Sun-egg, Svarog taught his son Svarozhich what was required. Svarog said to him, "Now of the dung of the golden-maned horse you shall knead clay and manufacture the rest of the world. It is for you to make this world orderly because I am all done." To emphasize this last point, Svarog gave a hearty yawn.

Svarozhich took his father's words to heart and obeyed the commands with the utmost care and diligence. The golden-maned horse dropped its dung, as warm and bright as fire. As this fire cooled, closely watched by the obedient Svarozhich, the world was gradually created from it. Svarozhich called on the other gods, all of those whom he had created out of the remains of his father's shattered leg, and with doubt and fear they watched him work.

Once the rest of the gods had gathered around, Svarozhich set loose two pigeons, one white and one black. The birds flew onto the cooled manure and began to fight. At first it seemed that the white bird was stronger, but a moment later the black bird would gain the upper hand, only to be beaten back again by the white. Neither bird could win, though, as they had both been sent by a god. Finally, Svarozhich stopped the struggle. Where the birds had fought the cooled manure had transformed. Everywhere that the feet of the white bird had touched had turned into fertile land, and everywhere that the feet of the black bird had touched had turned to rock and stone. Svarozhich put several final touches to the land, dividing hill from dale and creating rivers, streams, and even a large sea. He sent a strong, gusting wind over the sea to get clouds to rise off the surface and up into the sky. Svarozhich dispensed the very first rain on the earth. The beds of rivers and streams, springs and brooks pooled water, which turned many depressions, cracks, and gorges into bogs, marshes, and lakes.

But as the rivers and the sea were filling with water, Chaos made its appearance. At that moment, the rain water evaporated from the hot ground and the steam made the clouds so heavy they couldn't hold the water. Torrents of rain started to pour down on the land, overflowing the rivers and flooding the land. Now all was sea without shore, and even Svarozhich became scared. He was almost to the point of waking Svarog for help when the land rose up through the water, and he saw a myriad of creatures swimming in the seas and lakes and rivers. Plants burst from the rich, black soil, giving the earth a fresh green face. Reptiles, worms, and beetles were piercing and churning the dead clay. Both tame and wild animals made their way to the surface and spread out over the face of the world. Full of admiration and wonder, Svarozhich could not take his eyes off the wonders he had created. Mother Earth, gaining her power from the potency of the manure of the golden-maned horse and the heat from Svarog's heart, had managed to overcome the power of Chaos, that invincible force that always exists in the Universe.

Everything then seemed to develop as Svarozhich intended, with no peril in sight that could disturb his divine plan. But Chaos would not go away and admit defeat. It deliberately and malevolently mixed the clouds, causing catastrophic floods in some regions. Other areas, deprived of rain, were scorched until the ground cracked and everything that could move or grow was turned to dust. All life seemed doomed to perish. Once leafy forests and thickets were baking, and the once swarming animals were overwhelmed by the raging elements. What escaped the death of drought was scorched by the searing Sun. Where rain kept pouring down, the Sun's warmth could not reach the ground where it was so desperately needed.

Chaos bared his teeth and in a malignant grin aggravated the ordeal by inflicting a savage winter on the world. Chaos forbade the Sun to warm the ground. Animals were fleeing, searching for more hospitable areas.

Svarozhich contemplated the havoc Chaos had created in his world that had been bubbling with life and desperately tried to think of ways to curb the destructive force. While Chaos kept killing living creatures, Svarozhich tirelessly invented new and unusual plants and trees. Some could withstand clear skies, accompanied by heat and drought. Others, though shivering in the cold, were able to survive it.

After a time Svarozhich began to win in his battle with Chaos and overcome the disorder that had been created by promoting and enhancing new life. New plants and trees encouraged and hosted a vigorous animal life. Some of them sought the cold and water, while other could withstand incessant heat and drought. Svarozhich's combat with Chaos was long and difficult, but with the help of the other gods, he was able to overcome it.

But in no way does this mean that Chaos was defeated. The gods, gaining their strength from the mighty Svarog, had been able to keep Chaos in check. But Chaos kept testing them, contriving cunning new schemes in revenge. As soon as Svarozhich would fix one problem he would have to dash off to the ends of the earth to fix something else Chaos had destroyed.

This is when Svarozhich decided to assign four gods to rule the four quarters of the world. He chose the four wisest and most valiant of the gods as the kings of those regions. To help overcome Chaos, Svarozhich gave Perun, Radhost, Svantovit, and Dazhbog many of the same powers he had been holding for himself, even allowing them to assume his appearance and rule in his name when the need arose. Perun settled on the midnight side of the world, in the dankest and dingiest place of the earth, where Chaos would most frequently play havoc. Radhost set out for the evening side of the world, while Dazhbog went in the opposite direction, to the morning side. Svarozhich sent Svantovit to the southern regions, the midday quarter,

Svarozhich—Among Western Slavs, this deity was not only worshipped as the supreme god but was also seen as the personification of the Sun and fire. He was also invoked as a war god and a deity presiding over prophecies. He is thought of as the son of Svarog. People would bow down to him at the solstice and equinox, mainly because of their agricultural connections.

Fertility cult—was observed among the Slavic peoples who believed in the intimate relation between sex and the fertility of the ground. Its most vivid manifestations are to be found in heathen forms of sexual license, indulging passions to the fullest, amid song and dance and merrymaking involving particularly the young. We may assume that the profligacy which attended these ceremonies was an essential part of the rites. The union of the sexes was to ensure the fertility of nature. Ritualistically held,

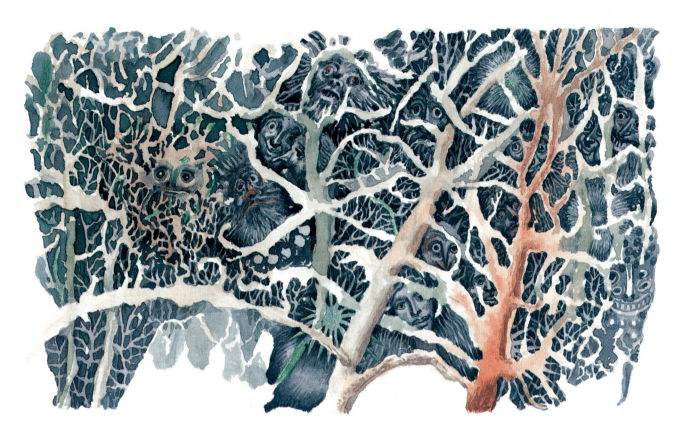

which is least tested by Chaos, so that he could give Svantovit, his favorite, many other duties as well.

The battle with Chaos continued for a long time, and many kinds of plants and animals were destroyed and created before a semblance of equilibrium was achieved and order was restored to the earth.

these orgies were much more than a mere outburst of unbridled passion. Love games survived well into the Middle Ages and even Modern times, though progressively waning and losing out to new cults and votive practices with the advent and advance of Christianity. The existence of fertility-cult is evidenced by surviving cultic objects including the well-known idol of Altfriesack with a special opening left for a phallus. This was attached to the statue during rituals and seasonal celebrations.

How
HUMANKIND
Came Into Being

Mother Earth, after the great struggle with Chaos, was given the name of Pripelaga by Svarozhich. But even after order had been restored, Pripelaga continued to feel miserable. Knowing this, Rod, a fertility god, approached her and said, "O divine Pripelaga, I do know you are in pain and your entire inside is burning. It's the Sun that is to blame for this flaming heat! Would you hug me? I will then let you in on a secret."

"What kind of secret? O Rod, I feel ghastly, you can hardly help me!" complained and groaned Pripelaga.

"It's the remainder of the fire from the hot manure of Svarozhich's horse with the golden mane that has been baking your insides. The horse pulls the Sun across the skies with Svarog, the one who has given you this lot of yours, sleeping inside. While he is sleeping, let me give you a piece of advice on how you could change this lot and put an end to your suffering," Rod said to her.

"What would you like me to do in return, I wonder? Well, I will not, so just come out with it! Do speak, right away, will you? O please, please, speak and help me!" entreated Pripelaga, wailing in pain.

"The burning won't subside," yelled Rod at the top of his voice, "unless you release from your belly creatures similar to the gods. But there is a catch, they must be at once mortal and immortal. Such is their lot. In my capacity as the fertility god I can advise that you try not to resist this lot that Svarog has given you. Each and every one of the creatures that you deliver is destined to die, unless

*P*RIPELAGA—*A deity worshipped by the Western, Polabian Slavs. The term includes tribes once settled between the rivers Saale, Elbe, the Baltic Sea, the Oder, and the Ore Mountains (Erzebirge), one of the most important tribal groups being the Lusatian Sorbs. The goddess controlled fertility. Legend ascribed to this deity the blood ritual of sacrifices made at her altar, a claim supported by surviving historical records. One of these is by Archbishop Adelgott of Magdeburg dating to 1108, where a parallel is drawn between Pripelaga and the ancient fertility god Priapus, son of Aphrodite (two of his reputed fathers being Dionysus and Pan). The procreative deity is commonly related to the idol of Altfriesack. Carved of oak, the statue features a head with an attempt at representing a hairstyle and an opening for an occasionally inserted phallus.*

granted immortality by the gods. But these creatures will attain immortality through the chain of their offspring, living in their children and their children's children. So, these creatures will multiply just like plants and animals. Almost god-like in appearance and deeds, they, nevertheless, will be doomed to live with the curse of their inevitable death."

Rod continued to talk to Pripelaga until he had convinced her that he was telling her the truth. Then, with the next surge of labor pains, she pushed forth from her complaining insides people. Their birth was accompanied by a deafening noise and an eruption of stones flying out of clouds of sulfurous smoke. The newly-born people were smeared in ash and were thirsty and hungry. Moreover, the newborn creatures knew nothing about the world they suddenly found themselves in. They were giants, standing so tall their heads nearly touched the clouds. They were made of clay with bones of stone, while their blood had been given by the sea and their eyes were given by sunshine. They had hair made of grass, but they were empty inside.

Svarozhich caught sight of these clay giants, god-like in appearance, yet so obviously not gods. Svarozhich took pity on them. But none of the other gods shared his sympathy for the creatures that looked so helpless. Svarozhich looked long and hard into the empty insides of the giants and saw that Chaos was there, searching for an opportunity. So Svarozhich drew a deep breath and breathed a gentle breeze into the giants, giving them a small piece of what the gods knew as eternity, and this is what gave the giants a soul.

The giants began to have children, and then their children had children of their own. With each successive generation the giants became smaller, and their clay and stones changed gradually into flesh and blood. Eventually the giants became extinct, replaced entirely by humans. After death these human people had to be committed to flames and burnt down to ashes or be buried in the soil in order to be returned to Pripelaga again. The soul alone does not belong to Mother Earth. Since Svarozhich had blown the soul into people, their souls return to him at death and are sent to the underworld realm of Veles.

While Svarozhich was blowing souls into the hollowness of the first people-giants, a very special noise was heard. Svarozhich came to realize that by his divine word, *slovo,* he had created the Slavic people. As the god wanted them to understand the meaning of this, he kissed them on their foreheads. It was this gesture that designated and made visible forever the residence of the human soul.

Under their forehead people have two apertures, a pair of eyes, windows for the soul to see and be seen. Two smaller openings, on either side of the forehead, have been designed for the soul to hear and listen. Placed between the eyes, there is a nose for discriminating smells. There is also a tongue for tasting all sorts of things, and, most importantly, below the nose people have a slot through which the soul, by means of the same tongue, speaks words of its own. People were to learn from the gods everything their divine models would choose and allow.

Pleased with this fine accomplishment, Svarozhich summoned the four divine kings, Perun, Svantovit, Radhost, and Dazhbog, together to celebrate. The gods quite enjoyed these new creatures, who ever after would become both sources of joy and fun as well as trouble and quarrels. The feast drew all of the lesser gods as well, and even Svarog longed to join them, and tossed restlessly in his bed. As Svarozhich looked out over the gods, it came to him that the time for a change had come.

Svarozhich then rose, and in a deep, resounding voice, proclaimed, "Our time is reaching its zenith! This is the Age of Dreams!" The other gods interrupted their feast. They understood that their main goal had been achieved, and that the Age of Dreams of the great Svarog was almost over. Despite the fact that they had been given souls and flesh and blood, humankind had not yet really lived. They simply slept at night and woke in the morning. They looked but they could not see, they pricked up their ears to catch sounds but could not truly hear. People

merged comfortably with the surrounding world and
nothing distinguished them from the animals. Mostly
these people just sadly watched life going on around them
and passing them by. They did not know that they were
living in the Age of Dreams.

THE GIANT OAK
the Abode of the Gods

After Svarog, the Father of the Gods, withdrew for his long sleep in the Sun, Svarozhich created the Giant Oak as the seat of the rest of the gods. The widespread roots stretch down deeply across the entire realm of Svarozhich, penetrating all of the four kingdoms divided among the divine kings. All four kingdoms feed the roots of the Giant Oak while the gods amuse themselves in the luxuriant foliage of the upper branches.

Perun, the divine ruler of the midnight kingdom, sits high in the Oak, hurling down his bolts of lightning. Radhost, dark-faced and raven-haired, gazes out upon his evening side, frowning at the Planetarians, the guardian spirits of the evening Auroras, as they light and watch the twinkling stars. Svantovit, Svarozhich's favorite, is seated on the afternoon side, while the handsome god Dazhbog takes his place beside Svarozhich on the morning side.

The gaze of the other gods is fixed on the main throne. They all have enormous respect for Svarozhich. Even Veles, the strong lord of the underworld, esteems Svarozhich. Zhiva, or Siva, the wife of Veles, is the goddess of love and death, and understands how these things are necessary in the human world. Their three sons, the divine princes Rugievit, Porenut, and Porevit, are the divinities of youthful athletic strength, as well as of warfare, and, unfortunately, imprudence and recklessness.

The aunt of these divine princes is Pripelaga, who is the goddess of the earth and fertility. She is frivolous and whimsical, a carefree goddess, while Mokosh, another fertility goddess and a bitter rival of Pripelaga, is dark and ominous.

SLAVIC PANTHEON—In conception and detail, the pagan nature worship of the Early Slavs shares the fundamentals of all great mythological systems. Like the Greeks, Romans and Teutons, the Slavs saw nature as animate and living. They saw natural forces as incarnated in mighty divine beings. The ancient Slavs believed that the sun, earth and water— the elements vital for their existence—were activated by invisible spirits, which prompted their worship and its multitudinous variety of forms, including sacrificial offerings. The Slavs associated the sound of the ripening crops as well as the rustle of a broad oak tree or a linden tree with demons and spirit- beings. They also believed the mighty oak tree to host in its trunk an invincible fertility god whose emblem was an acorn. The ancient Slavs made the flooring in their homes and ancillary structures of oak wood. Each tribe would reverence a divinity of its own, whom they honored by erecting a shrine or a temple of some kind. The study of polythe- istic systems has revealed that one and the same deity could appear in different places, assuming various guises. Moreover, such a deity was celebrated by local cults and customs,

31

and was called many parallel names deriving from its attributes. It was not unusual for the ancient Slavs to have a separate god for each region or even each settlement. The name of such a local divinity survived only if his or her impact spilt over the boundaries of a settlement or region and, above all, if immortalized by chroniclers. More often than not, however, the conceptions of Slavic gods would frequently blur and merge with their classical versions, both Roman and Teutonic. The Slavic pantheon featured its supreme and lesser gods. It was distinguished by mythic narrative mergers, hybrids and loans (mythological syncretism), particularly from the Roman pantheon, which had been in turn heavily influenced by Greek mythology. Slavic mythic narrative, then, could have drawn on Roman myths that had been adjusted to local needs and environment. Within the limits of the knowledge available today, it appears next to impossible to reconstruct in their entirety the myths of the early Slavs. No records testifying to the exchange between Classical and Slavic mythology have survived. The same holds good for the period of the progressive accommodation of Christian ideas and values by the heathen Slavs and their passage to monotheism.

Prove, Svarozhich's obedient servant, stands guard over law and justice. He is the father of the twin gods Sim and Rygl, who share one backbone. They can only move together, and their one body serves as a reminder that truth has at least two sides, just as their shared body exhibits two wills. For each notion the divine twins coin at least two expressions, as they view each event from at least two angles. Very often their views contradict each other, serving notice that wisdom can often assume apparently contentious forms. The way Sim and Rygl look also reveals considerable divergences. The two often appear as a horse with aquiline wings and one neck topped with two heads. But being gods, they can move independently of each other, though only in the Giant Oak. They also leave the tree often, most commonly in the guise of the wondrous and bizarre two-headed bird called Simargl.

Podaga, the weather-goddess, is also sprawled comfortably in the lush crown of the sacred oak tree. Podaga's son is Stribog, the god of air and winds. She also has four assistants and guardians, the demons of weather. These are Oblachnik the Cloud-Giver and Lord of the Winds, his wife Veternitsa the Wind-Bearer, his brother Frost, and the witch Yezhibaba or Baba Yaga.

Chors, the moon goddess, is nearby, as is Pizamar, the goddess of music and art. On another branch of the oak near them is Lada, the goddess of spring and beauty.

Another pair of divine twins, the goddesses Vesna and Morena, also reposes in the foliage of the Giant Oak. Vesna is the goddess of the Summer Solstice, as well as of spring and love, and is clad all in white. A smile invariably lights up her beautiful face, just the opposite of her sister. Morena the Pestilent is the goddess of the Winter Solstice and Death. She is constantly frowning and dressed in black funeral attire, giving her a morbid look. Morena had once gone to bed with Chernobog, the Black God of evil and bad luck, whom Svarozhich relegated to the lower branches of the Giant Oak, and borne a son, Triglav. The three-headed Triglav is the god of warriors and husbandry. He is greedy and ravenous; one head devours people, the second farm cattle, and the third fish.

Byelobog, the White God, also has a branch in the sacred tree. The other gods like teasing the venerable Byelobog, god of love, goodness, and forgiveness. The three divine brothers Rugievit, Porenut, and Porevit, along with their cousin, Yarovit, the god of military power and spring vitality, take special pleasure in baiting and playing tricks on Byelobog. Being kind-hearted, Byelobog cannot bear a grudge and always forgives the offenders. The loud and irrepressible laugh of Pereplut, the god of memory, can be heard as he enjoys the pranks of the brothers.

The sacred oak grows on the crossroads of the four worlds, the world of earth, the world of water, the world of air, and the world of fire, and is exposed to the hot rays of the Sun. In the winter the Giant Oak is tested by Frost, and has nothing to warm itself but a cloak of darkness by night and the demons of winds as they chase each other through the branches. Zora, the evening Aurora and her Planetarians and the Moon encourage the demons of the winds to eavesdrop on the gods as they race around the oak so that they can hear about the gods later.

The Giant Oak shelters all of the gods in its mighty branches that reach so high they comb the clouds. The roots run so deep into the earth that they reach the underworld realm of Veles. Harmony and disquiet alike reign in the oak. In times of beatitude and delight the gods are fond of listening to songs and pipe music while they drink milk and honey from horns and feast on mead and quass made from all the fruits of the earth. Beneath the Giant Oak is a grove of oak trees where the demons are allowed to gather. Though the demons are lesser divinities, they outnumber the gods three to one. Their purpose is to serve the gods and teach the people of the earth.

Kovlad the Iron-Keeper makes his bed under the Giant Oak. He is the mighty husband of the Mistress of the Earth, Runa, and the guardian of earthly treasures and caves. The mountain vile, dwarfish kobolds, Permoniks, the giant Ashliks, and Labus, the demon that lures children into tortuous caves, all serve Kovlad. In his home beneath the oak Kovlad meets with the other great demons such as

TRIGLAV—This god is a deity of the Polabian Slavs. Some researchers view his name as just another under which Svantovit was worshipped in the estuary of the Oder River, from where this god's cult spread all over what is now the Brandenburg province in Germany and surrounding areas. In Stettin (a present day territory in Poland) Triglav was represented, according to the written evidence of the twelfth century, by a blindfolded cultic statue with a golden belt covering his eyes and lips, supposedly to prevent him from seeing the sins of the people. The deity's three heads suggest the three spheres falling under his control—heaven, earth, and hell. Like many other ancient local divinities, Triglav was responsible for military matters and husbandry.

the King of Waters and Rivers and his wife, the Queen of Waters. Lesovik, the Lord of the Woods and the master of the woodland vile, also appears. The Lord of the Winds joins them, blowing and howling. The whole pack of the demons of fire show up, the brownies and dwarfs, Zmock, the Fiery Man, Bludichki, and Svetlonos. The majestic King of Time is there as well. Even the daughters of the god Prove, the Fates of Misery, Good Luck, and Revenge, and Kminska Kmotra the Thieving Godmother, with Death at her side, join in. The sylvan demons, Premien the Shape-Shifter, Mamuna, belching Grgalitsa, the Tatra Mountains woodland spirit, Boruta the Bark-Skinned, come together under the sacred oak. The quarrelsome field demons, Polevik, Rarashok, Hadovik, Pikulik, and Lasica, like to appear and bully the human-shaped demons.

Gazdichko-Domovik, Betiah-Madra, Mora the Nightmare, Vlkodlak, or Werewolf, Kikimora the Ugly Nuisance, the Planetarians, Vampire, and the phantom Babiak fight hard against each other, shrieking and screaming, disturbing the gods up in the crown of the tree. The superior gods warn the demons to keep quiet, sometimes resorting to hurling a bone down at them. If this fails, the gods pour hot mead onto the fighting tangle of spirits and dwarfs. The sticky mead always brings the mischievous demons to their senses and allows the gods peace to continue their feasting. Occasionally, when the gods grow bored in the Giant Oak, they invite a mortal up into the tree and reveal themselves to him and allow him to join in the feasting. Samo, the great king of the Slavs, is one of these mortals.

35   How the
AGE OF DREAMS
Came to Its End

The god Svarozhich created man, a Slav, by his godly word and a soul which he breathed into the clay giants. At first these people were content to sit in the oak grove beneath the Giant Oak and listen to the words of their gods. The gods reveled in the admiration of the people, letting them extol the virtues and miraculous deeds of the gods. The mortals beneath the tree lived a carefree life, never knowing hunger or thirst and never feeling cold or fatigue.

Yet the divine kings became anxious about the people, as they didn't want the people to feel that they, too, were gods. The gods took a special interest in the affairs of the mortals, and often quarreled among themselves about the events beneath the Giant Oak. They would get personally involved in the skirmishes and disputes, periodically helping the Fates and then obstructing them as the gods saw fit. Prove, the god of law and justice, had the enormous task of trying to keep order.

When Chernobog suggested that it was beneath the dignity of the gods to fight over the affairs of the mere mortals beneath the Giant Oak, the rest of the gods heartily agreed. Svarozhich then decided that the time had come to definitively end the Age of Dreams and complete the creation of the world.

During the Age of Dreams people existed rather than lived, locked into the pleasant cycle of sleeping and waking without knowing Good or Evil. They had lived comfortably with their natural surroundings, but now Svarozhich created the demons of Good and Evil. It was Evil that awakened the people and made them see just how different they were from the gods.

People thought the gods had ceased to love them, and it was Evil that helped the people try to protect themselves from the painful experience. Not knowing any better, the people looked for consolation in the lifestyle of the gods, yearning for the satiety and pleasure they had known before. But to experience these things people were forced to resort to evil practices, feeding and spreading Evil itself. They envied the gods and tried to imitate them, and Evil encouraged them, occasionally slipping the craving people crumbs that had fallen from the table of the gods. The people began to feel obliged to Evil for helping them ease their yearnings.

Finally, the gods turned the people away from the shadow of the Giant Oak, taking away the only protection the people knew. All of a sudden the people found themselves hungry and cold.

People then dwelt in the woods like animals, but lacked the claws and fangs of the beasts. The people were not as strong or fast as animals, and they had no fur to protect their naked bodies from the rain and cold. They did not boast the hooves given to animals or the wings given to birds, and the people had neither keen sight nor hearing, nor a fine and infallible sense of smell. People were not good at discerning edible roots from the poisonous fruits of the earth, and they knew of no way to protect themselves from cold or rain, darkness or drought. They slept in lairs from which they had turned out foxes and bears, trembling with fear that the animal would return to its stolen home. Fear also huddled them together in the pitch-black nights, which were occasionally pierced by the blood-freezing howls of wolves. Any unknown nook seemed like a nest of hissing snakes. The malicious and mischievous demons also robbed the people of the little rest they could find, as the demons were angry with the people for daring to live unprotected by the shadow of the Giant Oak.

Those first people lived as rivals with the animals for survival. They coveted the same food that the beasts did. Instructed by the sight of rodents digging out roots and nibbling at them with an appetizing crunch, the people began to dig up the edible roots. They carefully watched the beasts of prey, too, and learned how to chase and catch other animals, allowing the people to begin eating meat.

It was at this time that a nameless boy felt his time had come. In those earliest days, people were not simply given

names. They had to be named after an achievement or exploit, whether good or bad. Some people were even named after they had died. But this youth had a dream of doing a great deed, something that could help his family, as well as the family of the girl he loved.

The boy knew of an old tale of a tall magical plant with big sweet seeds. The tale said the ancient ancestors had discovered the plant on their long and difficult journeys in search of food. The legendary plant had been seen beyond the huge enchanted mountains, with their sharp peaks hidden in the clouds hovering between the midday and evening sides of the world. The coveted plant was believed to grow at the very edge of the world, on the bank of a wide river.

In vain the elders tried to dissuade the boy from undertaking the journey and wasting his life in its very prime, since bark-skinned Boruta, a capricious demon who was always on the hunt for people, lived in those high snow-covered mountains. No one that had ever ventured into those mountains had returned to see their families again.

Despite the cautions, the daring youth decided to go, and one night he bid farewell to his sweetheart and set out. After wandering for twenty-five days, the boy finally reached the mountains he had been seeking. The mountains were clad in a thick dull fog, a sure sign that Boruta was ready to stop intruders. Almost overcome by the cold and hunger, the young man slipped and stumbled along the steep slopes and trudged through waist-deep snowdrifts. Everything seemed to offer resistance to his passage. He did not even notice when or how he had managed to climb over the summit and down the other side.

But he had, and suddenly he found himself exposed to a completely unknown world. The deep snow, fierce winds, and gray fog had receded. He remembered all too well how cold and desperately hungry he had felt in the icy and jagged mountains, yet there on the other side everything was warmer and more comfortable. Even the pristine white snow didn't seem as cold. But this was not the end of the boy's journey. Heeding the advice of the elders, he went on, trying to find the spot that was exactly between the midday and evening sides of the world. He went on and on for such a long time that even-

*V*ELES—*The ancient Slavic deity was regarded as the patron of cattle and husbandry. He was responsible for crops, and the Slavs sought to ensure good harvests through a series of harvest time customs. He personified, above all, the fecundity forces which brought about increase in cattle and the annual success of the farmer's work in general. In time, Veles came to be the protector of animals and cattle. Following the adoption of Christianity, this god's functions were transferred to Saint Vlasil, while the Southern Slavs*

39

turned him into Saint Sava. Traces of Veles' cult are encountered in personal names, proverbs, and folk songs of the Fifteenth and Sixteenth Centuries. The god is depicted in Russian iconography surrounded by sheep, cows, and goats.

tually he began to despair of ever finding the wide river and magical plant bearing the big nourishing seeds.

The gods watched the wanderings of the intrepid youth closely. The farther the boy went, the angrier Veles grew, because the wondrous sweet plant was his property and he alone knew its secret. He doted on the plant and guarded it jealously, as it grew at the entrance to his underworld realm. But the boy kept pushing on, so Veles finally complained to the other gods. His divine peers ruled in his favor and gave Prove the task of setting an appropriate punishment to appease Veles. The punishment came from the King of Time. The youth, who was truly only a boy, suddenly began to grow old. Each day the King of Time would add new wrinkles to his face. His beard stretched down to his waist, his gait grew heavy and his back became hunched. The youth had not suspected what price he would have to pay for his daring deed, or how Veles would punish him for his audacity.

When he finally came across the vast field of waving golden plants, his looks had changed beyond recognition. His body had become totally emaciated. But it took him no time to realize that he had found what he was looking for, and the sight made his heart jump for joy. His lips trembled, but he uttered no words. Now, finally, he had stumbled upon the ripening plants full of milky golden grains. Eagerly he ate, and the more he partook of the wheat the less he remembered about his home. The Fate of Good Luck took pity on him and sent him a dream. He saw himself among his people, and they were suffering from hunger. They stretched out their empty hands to him, palms up, and their sunken eyes pleaded mutely. But he failed to recognize the people, even though some were his close family. Seeing this, Good Luck quickly took on the guise of his beloved and leapt into his dream. This shook the man from his slumber, and, wiping the sleep from his eyes, he jumped to his feet. Good Luck gave him will enough to overcome his fatigue and set out for home. Hurriedly, he plucked three dozen ears of the wondrous wheat and started for the mountains.

The man had been two days into his return journey to the jagged snowy mountains when Veles reprimanded the King of Time. The old man, once a daring youth, could barely walk. By then, however, the Fate of Good Luck had put in a good word for him with some of the other demons. March, the kind-hearted son of the King of Time, helped by giving an herbal potion to his father. Upon drinking it, the King of Time fell into a deep, three-month long sleep. Good Luck directed the brave man on the shortest path back to his home. She even pacified the whimsical snow storm, Metelitsa, who was wont to play havoc in those bleak mountains. The decrepit old man, cursed by the gods, still managed to find enough food and shelter along his journey to keep him alive. He had been gone for over twelve months, and all that time his people had mourned his loss.

Finally, more dead than alive, the man found himself within a half-day's walk of his home and village. Tired but happy, he stopped for a short rest before taking the final walk. He knelt to wash his face in a spring, and he did not recognize his own reflection. He wept bitterly, wondering how he would appear to his beloved.

Yet the Fate of Good Luck, having helped him so much already, could not leave him in trouble. She persuaded Kikimora, who is known for taking delight in harming people of both sexes, that by transforming the old man into a youth, Kikimora would make two women unhappy, the wife of the old man and the girl who would mistake him for her beloved. Good Luck then breathed on the old man to make him fall asleep. When he awoke, his beard, wrinkles, and the heavy gait of old age were gone. Even all of his teeth had grown back. Overjoyed, the youth raced home to his loved ones with the grain, which they were able to sow, harvest, thrash, rind, and bake into bread. Since the grain had come from the gods, it was named "zbozhi," the crop of the gods. Further, the people all agreed that the youth had performed a great feat, and he was given the name Slav, in honor of all the Slavic people that the grain would help.

Just as the first word through which Svarozhich had breathed a soul into the emptiness inside man had begun the Age of Dreams, so the first human tear began the Stone Age. It was a simple tear falling in anguish from the eye of the old man that taught people to fear the gods and be humble. People revered the gods and worshipped them, wanting to learn their secrets. But the gods jealously guarded the secrets of fire, time, fertility, the taming of animals, and many others in those first years of the Stone Age, causing the people immense hardship.

CHAPTER 2

The Stone Age

SVAROZHICH
the Intrepid Warrior

Svarozhich, the lord of the world, was busy in the beginning of the world helping the earth goddess Pripelaga overcome the forces of Chaos. But during this struggle the invincible Chaos managed to steal a portion of the strength of the gods and create demons of his own, and it was these malevolent demons that caused the great deluge and almost destroyed the world.

But Chaos and his demons didn't like the fact that they had been beaten by Svarozhich and tried to find a way that they could take control of the world. Chaos decided that to defeat Svarozhich he would have to gain control of the Sun-egg, since Svarog, the Father of the Gods, could offer no resistance in his sleep.

Svarozhich woke one morning and went to the Milky Way, where his golden-maned horse liked to graze. The god patted it affectionately and smoothed its mane before harnessing it to the delicate celestial chariot. They sped off at a full gallop, racing the whirlwind Vikhor, all the way to the edge of the world. There Svarozhich rolled the glowing Sun-egg into the chariot and leapt in himself to start the climb across the sky.

As Svarozhich approached the horizon, he knew he must be extremely careful. That is the point where he is the most vulnerable and may at any moment be assaulted by the evil demons who have collectively assumed the shape of the ill-natured Chmarnik. This arch-demon of the clouds is notorious for killing people at whim.

There are days when the wicked demons dare not attack Svarozhich. On these days the morning sky is as clear as crystal. Only the light, powdery clouds tended by the benevolent demon Pohvizd the Whistler can be seen as they bask in the blue sky. Sometimes mischievous Oblachnik the Cloud-Bringer, Pohvizd's son and Podaga's lazy grandson, grazes the celestial cloud flocks. Oblachnik is apprenticed to Pohvizd, the father of the winds and the shepherd of the shy white clouds. But there are many days that Pohvizd dares not send his lambs to graze, but rather drives them to shelter. These are the days when Chmarnik chooses to stretch his dirty, obnoxious cloak of smoke, fog, and darkness all over the skies. This is when evil Chmarnik assaults Svarozhich and tries to capture the Sun, the source of all life on earth.

The only thing Svarozhich can do is fight Chmarnik. The arch-demon Chmarnik is a huge winged dragon with a vulture-like body and a chest made of iron. He has long, sharp claws and three heads with flint beaks filled with razor-sharp, poisonous teeth. His mouth and nostrils breathe and spit blood-red flames and suffocating sulfurous smoke. When he flaps his enormous wings the entire sky shivers, and each movement raises pillars of dust and drives the clouds. One swipe of the monster's tail shrouds the world in thick fog.

Chmarnik's goal is to peck out the eyes of Svarozhich and to tear the golden-maned horse to pieces. Then he would grab the Sun-egg in his horrific talons and take it to the darkest part of the Universe, where the malevolent demons impatiently wait to lock Svarog in their dungeon.

With so much at stake, the evil Chmarnik jumps out to stop the chariot. The golden-maned stallion rears up and neighs wildly, keeping his hooves up, ready to fight. Svarozhich draws his shimmering golden sword. Chmarnik knows to fear the mighty sword, yet the sword alone is not enough to defeat him. Svarozhich would be able to smite one of the heads, but then Chmarnik's other two would surely peck out the eyes of the god. But the golden-maned horse will not let Svarozhich fight alone, and astounds Chmarnik by assuming the shape of a golden hound.

The clever hound attacks and baits the dragon, allowing Svarozhich the opportunity to take a mighty swing and cut off one of the three hideous heads. But Chmarnik

doesn't give up, and one of his heads assails Svarozhich while the other attacks the golden hound. And worse yet, Chmarnik draws his necks inside his body, making himself invincible from the front.

The battle rages on until Svarozhich is very nearly exhausted. Fiery tongues of his hot sweat flow off the god, and it seems that he may not be able to win this contest. At that moment, the magical hound changes its shape again, this time into a furious golden bull. The shiny horns of the bull infuriate Chmarnik, and he carelessly exposes a second neck in his rage. Svarozhich quickly swings his golden sword and hacks off a second head. Even with only one head left, Chmarnik can still watch Svarozhich and the golden bull. Both are exhausted.

Pulling in his third neck, Chmarnik soars upward, sending shivers through the sky. The warriors are shrouded in a cloud of dust and smoke. Chmarnik comes flying back down through the smoke to attack with his talons. The fighting is savage and desperate. The bull, badly wounded, drops down on its front knees as blood trickles from all over his body. It cannot continue the fight. Svarozhich, too, is bleeding all over and running out of strength. He can barely dodge the vicious blows of the dragon's talons. Now Chmarnik employs another of his terrible weapons. Instead of blood he has a deadly tar running in his veins, which spouts from his wounds. Chmarnik aims the stumps of his chopped-off heads and sprays the hot tar at Svarozhich, and it is all Svarozhich can do to get out of the way.

The bitter contest is culminating with a dreadful end in sight. Just when Chmarnik is moving in to finish off Svarozhich, a golden rooster comes to the rescue. This is the same bird that used to watch over the golden-maned horse before Svarozhich captured it. Now the rooster lets out its shrill cry. Taken aback, Chmarnik turns his head in the direction of the belligerent sound. Confused, the dragon forgets to keep his last neck pulled in. But Svarozhich can no longer raise his golden sword, much less swing it to chop off Chmarnik's last head. And the bull is down on its knees, bellowing in pain. Its bloodshot eyes can barely see anymore. Yet the beast makes a final effort to stagger to its feet, and, mustering every last ounce of its strength, furiously charges the dragon.

The bull's courage and daring fill Svarozhich with new strength. He draws his sword and starts forward. Chmarnik is just about to turn back to the god when the bull drives its horn up through the jaw of the last head. Chmarnik twists and pulls to try to protect his neck again, but each movement just drives the horn in deeper. Bleeding tremendously, Svarozhich raises his sword high and lets it drop, severing the third head of the evil Chmarnik.

The entire Universe shakes and shivers throughout. The malevolent demons let out a moan. The arch-demon Chmarnik, with his headless body, is put to flight.

Indignant and humiliated at the same time, he spreads his wings and leaves the site of the lost battle. Guided by his faultless instinct, Chmarnik flies straight to the dark part of the Universe where the other demons wait for him. His three heads will grow back by the following day and his wounds will heal, leaving him ready to resume the battle.

Meanwhile, the golden rooster carefully collects in his beak some honeyed milk from the Milky Way and gently lets it drop into the mouths of Svarozhich and the golden bull. In no time their wounds have healed, and the two forget not only their sores but also their gallant deeds. The day is drawing to a close, and they continue on with the golden chariot. The evening visage of the two-faced Aurora, the Evening Star, has already appeared to celebrate the sunset by singing.

How the Gods Started
HELPING PEOPLE

At first the people feared the gods rather than loved them. It was more out of awe than respect that they made offerings to the gods, trying their best to not upset the immortals. But it was Perun, the fearsome god of thunder, who, quite by accident, first earned the love of the people.

Some of the goddesses in the Giant Oak were amorous and seductive beauties known for their sensual pursuits. This displeased Svarozhich, so he commanded them to restrain their unbridled indulgences and wait for love to come to them. This meant being patient throughout the winter and waiting for someone to approach them in the spring.

Svarozhich's command notwithstanding, young Vesna, the goddess of spring, wasted no time luring Perun himself into the snares of love. She refused to wait until the arrival of spring to start weaving a delicate web of temptation around Perun. In a moment of weakness, the god of thunder gave up his resistance and moved to put his arm around Vesna. Before he could, though, he had to free his hands, which meant hurling the bolt of lightning he had been holding down at the earth. This produced a peel of thunder that heralded the end of winter, the season in which Morena the Pestilent reigned over the earth.

This first clap of thunder awakened all the elemental gods and demons. Mokosh, Pripelaga, Zhiva, Yarilo, the three divine brothers Rugievit, Porenut, and Porevit as well as the demons of earth, water, fire and air suddenly woke up. Even the woodland demons and spirits of the field could hear the call to wake up from the long winter. The call was the voice of the superior gods, Dazhbog,

Svantovit, Perun, and Radhost, as they whispered, "Wake up, everybody! The season of the bleak sleep and deadly rest is over!"

When the people discovered that Perun, in Vesna's embrace, held the power to awaken new life, they longed to shorten the period of cold sleep. With that in mind, people set up the first crude shrine to the god of thunder. They simply fenced in an oak tree grove, knowing that oaks were Perun's favorite trees, to protect the trees and thus please Perun. They even appointed a guard for the sacred grove, and gave the guard the duty of pleading to Perun on behalf of the people.

It didn't take long for the other gods to become jealous of the adoration Perun was receiving. Mokosh, the goddess of fertility, was the first to do something about it. She took on the guise of a lovely girl and seduced a young man, Mitran. Knowing that she was pregnant, Mokosh then went to her father, Rod, the god of fertility, to ask him to hasten the delivery. Before daybreak Mokosh had given birth to a boy. By noon of the same day the child had grown into an adult. By nightfall this first demigod, half god and half human, became the first official priest, and was called Mokosits. It was his sacred function to pray to Mokosh alone as the goddess of fertility, patron of weavers, and protector of sheep, as well as to spread her glory to the people. He would make blood sacrifices in her honor on a large stone beneath a tall linden tree. While supplicating the goddess to foster the growth of crops, he would cut the throats of sheep, wash his face and dip his hands up to the elbows in the steaming blood, then kneel down and piously kiss the ground. To finish the ritual, he would lie prostrate on the earth and spread his arms wide in a symbolic gesture of embracing Mother Earth as the true mother of all. Mokosh, in reward for his devotion, would visit the priest in his dreams. As the weaver goddess, she taught the priest how to shear sheep, wash the wool, and spin threads on a spinning wheel.

Chagrined, the god Stribog was the first to complain. The lord of air and wind, Stribog, was jealous of Perun's grove and the priest of Mokosh. He asked Svarozhich to

MOKOSH—*The only goddess from the Russian pantheon known from a chronicle and tracts written between the tenth and twelfth centuries. In more recent folk sources, the goddess is invoked as protector of sheep and patron of spinners. She is the deification and personification of moist fertile soil—the "mother benefactress" so dearly loved by every Slavic farmer. The name of this goddess also appears beyond the eastern Slavic region in, for example, Slovak surnames or in the local name of a mountain peak in the Czech Republic.*

punish Mokosh for her audacity by killing the demigod Mokosits. Svarozhich himself was very angry with Mokosh and slowly rose to his feet. He was about to rain fire down on the oak tree and cromlech where Mokosits lay sleeping when Mokosh threw herself at the feet of Prove, the god of justice.

"O Prove, I pray you, help me!" she cried.

Prove, however turned away both of his faces. As sorry as he felt for the desperate mother, the god of justice could not let her offense go unpunished.

But the delay allowed Svarozhich time to think. He raised his right hand. "Very well! It would do no harm if the people were to show more reverence toward us. I won't kill your son. But I must punish your misdeed, Mokosh, since you are the first to commit such an offense. Therefore, Mokosits, your child, will live forever on the edge between life and death. In lieu of Simargl, he will be the servant of Veles and the keeper of the entrance gate to the netherworld. He will graze Veles' cattle and look after the magical plant that Veles grows on the bank of his river, which people have already stolen once. As for the bloody offerings, these shall be held to honor the highest gods alone."

Since Svarozhich's decree people have worshipped Mokosh by crumbling food and pouring libations. The first drop from the first cup was to be spilled on the ground and the first crumb of the first mouthful had to be flung over the left shoulder as the offerings made to both Mokosh and another goddess of fertility, Pripelaga. But it was the disclosure of the secret of sheep's wool, as well as those of spinning and the spinning wheel, which earned Mokosh the admiration of the people. Seeing this, the other gods were jealous and wanted sacred sites, altars, and priests devoted solely to them. To gain loyalty and devotion from the people the gods began to give people small gifts, things that made the lives of their worshippers less difficult.

Prove, for one, taught people to care for justice and to respect and obey laws. He persuaded people that they might not harm anyone who had taken refuge within a sacred enclosure of oaks. Svantovit taught people the craft of divination and soothsaying. Triglav endowed people with the invention of the wheel. Yarilo instructed them in how to sharpen stone and till the soil. Podaga gained worshippers by revealing the secret of weather forecasting. Pizamar gave people one of her melodious pipes and taught them music and other arts. Byelobog revealed the healing properties of herbs, showing them which ones were good for treating cuts and which ones could be chewed to relieve pain. Veles also wanted a shrine, so he taught people how to milk animals. Dazhbog showed people how to build homes, which allowed them to come

*P*ROVE—*This god was a tribal deity of Polabian and Baltic Slavs. He was worshipped mainly in Wagria (in present day Germany), which was the westernmost Slavic land. The deity ruled over the "Oldenburg land," the Slavonic name being "Starigrad," or "old town." A sacred oak grove was dedicated to this god. The deity appears not to have been associated with any well-known cultic figurine. His rites were performed in the oak grove, and this hallowed spot was accessible only to the priest who performed the sacrifice, a worshipper intending to make a votive offering, or a wayfarer or a runaway seeking sanctuary.*

out of the caves they had been living in. Chernobog longed to be worshipped, so he secretly taught people how to hunt animals and set traps. Rugievit granted them a spear, Porenut a bow with arrows, and Porevit gave an axe.

In this manner each of the gods would let out the knowledge that was supposed to have been reserved for the gods alone. Yet with these gifts, the gods gave people something else as well. People were given a chance of transcending their mortality through great deeds and heroic acts that would live forever in the grateful memory of the living. With the blessings dispensed by the gods, the fortunes of humankind began to change for the better.

ll of the gods envied Svarozhich his stallion with the golden mane. As Svarozhich drove the Sun across the sky he was careful to take his time, as each journey had to take exactly one day. But every now and then, particularly on bright summer days, when people worked hard in their fields and frequently had to wipe the streaming sweat from their faces, the god would stop. Then Svarozhich would unhook the chariot and hop on the back of the stallion and take a good, wild ride. Dashing around on the golden-maned horse, Svarozhich's voice would boom across the sky in joy. It was these moments of utter happiness as he rode his horse that drew the envy of the other gods.

There was nothing that could have made Svarozhich give up his horse. The faithful stallion was always the first to sense danger and no trick of fate, not even the intrigue of the other gods, could make the horse unaware. It was not due to chance but rather Fate that horses came to be perceived as the symbol of strength and vigor, and all horses are descended from the golden-maned stallion of Svarozhich.

The other gods were only too aware of the attributes of the horse and made up their minds to have horses of their own. The gods searched all corners of the earth, from the thick forests to the dry deserts, for the finest stallions. They captured and tamed those horses and put saddles on them, keeping them secretly in the leafy sacred groves and shrines set up in honor of the individual gods, charging the priests with the care of the horses.

Radhost kept such a horse in remote Rethra, a place in the extreme corner of the lands settled by the Slavs.

Svantovit had several horses, which were used in fore-telling the future, but he kept his favorite at the sanctuary at Arcona. Rugievit was very proud of his two horses, which came from Volgast and Korenica. Triglav kept his horse in Stettin. Perun would often go as far away as Kiev to ride his spirited stallion. The amusing and frivolous god Yarilo would lend his black horses to the priestess at Devin. Dazhbog was known to hide his horse at Hvar, while Prove kept his in Nitra and Stribog at Velehrad, far beyond Moravske Mesto. The gods kept all of this away from the eyes of Svarozhich, knowing that he felt that his possession of the golden-maned stallion was a privilege due only to the king of the gods. They were afraid to make him angry, let alone offend him by daring to mimic him.

Yet there is nothing that can be hidden from the keen eagle eye of Svarozhich. He summoned the other gods and breathed a sigh of rage.

Svantovit was the first to think of an excuse. He said, "You are right. I am taming and training a horse of my own," when Svarozhich reprimanded him. "I am doing this so that I may afterwards hand the horse over to the people. Why, each god has divulged one of our divine mysteries to them. Some even two or three of these."

"Without ever bothering to have my consent!" Svarozhich roared back.

"Yet none has taught them how to read the future. Not in the least. They act and behave as if they were blind," continued Svantovit.

"And what?" muttered Prove sheepishly.

"Don't you know that destiny issues from the will of the Father of All Gods, Svarog?" asked a horrified Svarozhich. "The last thing we need is to have any of us negotiating immortality with those people! Am I right in understanding that you are looking forward to inviting those miserable earth creatures to share in our feasts here in the Giant Oak?"

"I'm ever so sorry, Svarozhich," said Chors, "but I have taught them to sing and recite poems, and . . ."

"Poems and songs are exclusively divine business. People will never learn to truly appreciate such things," grumbled Svarozhich.

"Do you think the wheel is too big a boon to give to people?" Triglav asked to defend himself.

"You know best how big it is," Svarozhich retorted, and reaching down, he angrily snapped off one of Triglav's heads.

Disgusted, Svarozhich leaned back and thought about what he should do, half-heartedly listening as the gods continued to bicker like children. Each tried to play down his or her own offenses so that those of others might stand out more glaringly. Yarilo made jokes about the grinding of flints and hoes and spades, Podaga murmured that the signs of bad weather and rain were not secrets for long, even to young children, and Pizamar made a shy remark about the art of calling sounds from a pipe. Byelobog challenged the healing effects of herbs, Dazhbog doubted the utility of 'zemliankas,' the shelters he had taught people to build, and Veles, all of a sudden questioned the benefits of milking animals. Following the lead of the others, the divine brothers Rugievit, Porevit, and Porenut unanimously dismissed the value of their boons—the spear, the bow, and the axe. Only Chernobog kept silent, and stood grinning.

"Peace!" Svarozhich shouted at them. "And you, stop grinning!"

"Excuse me, Highest One," ventured Chernobog, raising his hand. "But let me say this. For myself, I do stand up for the gifts I have given the people. In no event do I regret doing so."

"Your boasting is the last thing I want to hear," Svarozhich said angrily in another attempt to silence Chernobog.

But Chernobog was determined to finish. "There is no denying that all these gifts are precious information and the most guarded mysteries, yet they still remained mysteries, because only the gods can handle them properly. Otherwise these gifts might turn against the very people that would put them to use. I have also given people gifts. I have shown them how to chase game and helped them develop the skills they need for successful killing. Ha-ha! Do you believe that people will wield these gifts only for

CHERNOBOG (The Black God, 'cherni' means 'black' and 'bog' is the Slavic equivalent of 'god')—This god was the epitome and personification of evil forces and the dark side of life. This malevolent divinity is referred to in accounts of great feasts. Depicted as a dark figure dressed all in black, he had as his counter-part Byelobog, the White God, who personified all things good. Particularly feared in northern Russia with its long periods of seasonal darkness, this deity is referred to by a priest named Helmold. In 1155-1156 he accompanied his mentor, Bishop Gerold of Oldenburg, on his mission to Slavic Wagria. Helmold relates a native Slavonic custom of generous libations to appease the dreaded deity Chernobog.

their benefit? The wheel, flints, the hoe and spade, even
the ability to read the signs of weather will turn against
them if they do not duly respect and guard these advantages.
They will be punished by their own folly and impudence.
Ha-ha!" he laughed again.

The gods lapsed into silence. They stopped quarreling,
and even Svarozhich did not seem angry any more. They
decided to allow Svantovit to give people at least a tiny
portion of the skill of seeing the future. People would be
allowed to cross lances on the ground, and then the fortune-
telling horse would step over them. If the animal were to
start with the left leg, it would be a caution that the war
might not be successful, and perhaps they should seek
peace.

"Very well," Svarozhich finally agreed. "But it must be
a different sort of horse, different from mine and also
from ordinary horses."

Svantovit solved the problem quite easily. He gave the
horse neither a different head, nor tail, nor ears, nor even
mane. He changed only one simple thing to comply with
Svarozhich's order. The gods were astonished to see
Svantovit lead out the prophetic horse, which was completely snow-white.

Nobody else was allowed to possess such a horse. Just
as there is only one horse with a golden mane, nobody
was supposed to imitate Svantovit's white horse. This
was a law that was understood among the gods, yet even
those laws are stretched and broken once in a while. It
was none other than the lusty Yarilo, god of fertility and
merrymaking, who tried this unwritten law. Yarilo,
drunk as usual from his merry feasting, dared to saddle
his light gray—almost white—horse, leap on it, and gallop
proudly at the head of his humorous train. Exuberant
crowds of people were at that time giving themselves to
wild merrymaking and feasting, which allowed Yarilo to
get away with his impudence. Being what he was, though,
Yarilo would also lend his horse to the priestess at Devin,
as Yarilo knew best where the fairest and most appealing
maidens in the world would gather to sing and dance in a
ring.

How
PIZAMAR
was Granted Immortality

Svarozhich, the ruler of the gods, tried his best to play his lordly part as the demanding, revered, and even feared celestial king. But Svarozhich held no illusions about the divine occupants of the Giant Oak. He knew that the other gods really only obeyed his commands when it suited them and that behind his back they behaved as they pleased, even when acting in opposition to his orders.

Despite his own bans on intemperate love affairs, Svarozhich himself would now and then succumb to wild sensual calls. It so happened that a matchless and irresistible beauty called Pizamar won, unknowingly, Svarozhich's divine affection. Pizamar came from the lands beyond the banks of the blue Danube River, in the heartland of the area settled by the Slavs.

Day by day, Svarozhich, the heavenly charioteer and highest deity, surveyed the Slavic lands from the heights of the sky and nothing could escape his gaze. The bored god would look for something that might please his eye and add excitement to his routine journey across the dome of the world. Svarozhich observed the eternal gamut of joy and sadness, faithfulness and treacherousness, birth and death, affection and hatred, abundance and famine, good and evil, wealth and poverty, as well as gold and filth. He would smile at the sight of beauty and become sad when perceiving evil. Modesty pleased him, whereas he swallowed a bitter lump when he saw arrogance, violence, and excessive pride. Svarozhich did care for the people, even the 'Nemtsi,' those who lived outside the Slavic world.

What he enjoyed most, however, was to search for the wide blue ribbon of the Danube River as it cut its way through the very middle of the Slavic world. Beyond one of the tributaries he once happened to catch sight of a maiden whose beauty surpassed that of any other woman ever born. In humble garb, she seemed content to just breathe and sing, and looked miles away from wanting either riches or high honors. Pizamar was her name, and she was the youngest of seven daughters of a base farmer and fishmonger, who had hoped to be blessed by at least one son. Pizamar was of a mortal mold, not the celestial material with which Svarozhich had created the gods.

It is impossible to say whether it was by chance or by the hand of the Fates that Svarozhich saw Pizamar again. While the first time Svarozhich had simply feasted his eyes upon her beauty and the wonder of her ways, the second and third times Svarozhich laid his eyes on her he was smitten with her youthful beauty. If, on the following days, she stayed in by chance, he found his thoughts drawn to her and his eyes impatiently searching for her. Perplexed, Svarozhich noticed that he even started to worry about her and could not banish thoughts of her from his mind. He needed to know her whereabouts. Charming Pizamar went on singing by the river, completely unaware she had attracted someone of such stature.

Consumed by desire, the lovesick god laid his plot. In the guise of a sunbeam, he suddenly and affectionately embraced Pizamar's young, lean body and lightly caressed her lovely face. That frightened the girl and a shudder went through her body, yet she didn't want it stop, even though she didn't know what was happening. At other times Svarozhich would go to her as a mist coming off the lazy flow of the river or else as a simple breeze. Oblachnik, the Lord of the Winds, frequently punished this breeze for taking such license with the mortal, not knowing that the breeze was really Svarozhich himself. And on still other occasions Svarozhich would go to her as a mere fragrance, but each time he left her pregnant. Afterwards Svarozhich would be ashamed of his weakness and conduct as the ruler of the gods. Therefore, all of his children were doomed to be born

60

*P*IZAMAR—*This deity and her cult are supported by almost no artifacts or direct written reference. Existing historical records allow us to assume that the worship of this goddess was spread across Yasmund, the north-eastern part of legendary Rujana, generally considered to be the present day Rugen Island and the nearby coastal areas. Her idol appears to have been burnt there around 1168.*

dead. As the king of the gods, Svarozhich would not let demigods be born through his consorting with Pizamar, and, though he suffered pangs of remorse, each morning he could not help himself and would go to her again.

Pizamar grew very sad because of this. Her former youthful vigor had disappeared, and her rolling tears were very often her only nourishment. All alone she grieved, walking to the edge of a high cliff overhanging the river and wishing herself dead. One of the demons that served Veles, Death, was already waiting for Pizamar's body in the cold waves beneath the cliff. The demon's fleshless bones rattled with anticipation. Mokosits had his bag ready to drop in her coin so he could unlock the creaking gates to the underworld realm of Veles for her. But Svarozhich's divine conscience was not entirely asleep. He taught Prove's daughters, the Fates, how to avert Pizamar's death. Whenever the young woman went up on the cliff, they called Nochnitsa, the Night Fairy. Nochnitsa would make Pizamar very sleepy every time she went near the cliff, and, overwhelmed by drowsiness, the girl would fall asleep on the spot, preventing her from taking that last step.

The goddess of spring and love, Lada, also beautiful in form and aspect, could not bear to see Pizamar suffering so profoundly. Even the pining Chors could not help but fall in love with the fair girl who reminded the mourning Chors of her own lost daughter. It was finally Chors, heeding Lada's urging, who suggested to Svarozhich how to put things right again.

"Why don't you grant her immortality?" she whispered to Svarozhich. "I could help you by stealing it for Pizamar. But promise me that afterwards you will be on my side in court and put in a word for me with the gods. Don't let Prove banish me into your disgrace and hand me over to the demons of Evil."

Svarozhich was at a loss. He still could not help going to the beautiful Pizamar, yet he was making her profoundly unhappy. Still beauteous to behold, she nevertheless could not hide her suffering from the eyes of her family, and she was not herself anymore. The elders even began to suspect her of consorting with Chernobog and other malevolent spirits.

In the end, Svarozhich decided that Chors was right. Mead, made of honey gathered by divine bees, was watched over by the goddess Podaga. To get it away from her, Svarozhich had to seduce Podaga while Chors slipped past and stole some of the precious mead. Long after, Podaga was suspicious of any who tried to win her affection.

But with the mead in her possession, Chors went to Pizamar. While the young girl slept the goddess dipped the potion of the gods into the soul of the girl. Pizamar's soul then shone so brightly that it could not enter the kingdom of Veles, just as the rays of the Sun and Moon were forbidden the underworld, since the light would disturb the souls of the dead. Soon after, Svarozhich ordered Veles to remove the palm print of Pizamar from the wall of his dark cave. Without the palm print, Death had nothing to rely on to identify a mortal, and the last threat to Pizamar's eternal life was removed for good.

Fair Pizamar was given a place in the crown of the Giant Oak by Svarozhich, who acted as though nothing special had happened. A wave of his hand was enough to stop the grumbling of the other gods. And Pizamar became even more beautiful. She would smile and take out her pipe and play tunes for the other gods, and the frowns would disappear. Entranced and softened by her music, even Chernobog would close his eyes, and the evil that was forever in his soul would lie dormant for a time. To save himself further trouble, Svarozhich appointed Pizamar the goddess of the arts, music, and harmony.

Of the
THREE DIVINE BROTHERS

It was not merely the gifts of the spear, bow, and axe which earned the three brothers the worship of the people. Rugievit, Porenut, and Porevit are true brothers in every sense of the word. They always work together, epitomizing the three prerequisites of any successful undertaking, namely wisdom, strength, and beauty.

Rugievit is all strength. He has seven faces, one next to the other and all squeezed together under his crown. He is also armed with seven swords in his belt and an eighth one in his right hand. The seven attributes of strength, swiftness, endurance, maneuverability, robustness, dynamism, implacability, and the will for victory, are each represented by a face. Not particularly handsome, Rugievit prefers to withdraw to the sacred grove in Rujana when he is not engaged in chases or battles.

The middle brother, Porenut, personifies wisdom. While Rugievit has seven faces, Porenut has five. All are sly visages, able to watch for danger from all directions at once. The fifth, however, stems from his chest. Even if Porenut were to have his throat cut, his brains, the source of his wisdom, would remain with his body. Porenut usually rubs his forehead with his left hand while the right supports his chin. A thinker and tinkerer in one, it is Porenut who invented the bow and arrow.

The cousin of the three brothers is Yarovit, who is jealous of the wisdom of Porenut. He likes to amuse himself by playing mischievous pranks on Porenut, and Porenut always does the same to Yarovit. The other gods get tremendous enjoyment out of the tricks the cousins like to play on each other.

RUGIEVIT (Rugjevit, Rijevit, or Rugavit)—A seven-headed deity of the Slavic tribal group called the Runi (who once inhabited the territory of present day Germany). He appears to have been a war god, hence he has been compared to Mars, the ancient Roman god of war, identified in turn with the Greek god Ares. This figure of the Slavic pantheon is depicted with eight swords and his cult probably developed from tales of a legendary tribal chieftain. His cult centered on the settlement of Garz, in what was once known as Rujana. The description of his idol is a statue that was so tall that when Bishop Absolon stood at its feet, he could not reach the idol's beard even with his axe.

The youngest of the brothers is Porevit. He also has five faces, one gentle, one like a mirror, one painted, one merry, and the last capricious. Each is attractive in its own way and all are equally admired by the goddesses. But the handsome Porevit has to take care not to over-shadow Dazhbog, since this mighty god can stand no rivals when it comes to his beauty. Therefore the goddesses are careful to divide their attentions between the elder and mightier Dazhbog and the youthful Porevit in such a way that neither feels neglected.

As the three brothers grew up, like other young brothers, they would periodically fight each other. Upon noticing the seeds of animosity growing between the elder two, Veles made up his mind to nip the rivalry in the bud.

So Veles sent Rugievit and Porevit off on a hunt, while he made Porenut stay home. Then Veles took the guise of an eagle to lure the two hunters. Although Rugievit could throw his spear almost as well as Perun could hurl light-ning, it was of no avail with the eagle. Likewise, Porevit had no success with his golden axe. The eagle merely took to the sky and disappeared.

"We would be very lucky to be able to hit a bird without Porenut's bow and arrows," the two brothers agreed as they set out for home with nothing to show for their hunt.

"Where is your eagle, I wonder?" Veles said to tease them.

The next day, Porenut and Porevit were sent hunting while Rugievit stayed home. This time Veles took the shape of a mighty auroch. Its fur was thicker than a boar's tail and its skin was harder than the bark of a hundred-year-old oak tree, and the animal had all of Veles' strength.

Porenut's unerring and numerous arrows flew at the auroch, but merely glanced off the animal's thick hide. Seeing that, Porevit fell upon the bison, but whenever he drew close enough to use his axe, the auroch would turn on him and drive him away. Even Porenut's wisdom was of no avail, as the auroch faultlessly avoided every trap and stratagem the two brothers tried. Eventually they had to return home with nothing to show for the day's hunt.

As derisive as before, Veles scolded the hunters for coming home empty-handed.

On the next day Veles sent the strong Rugievit and the wise Porenut out to hunt. This time it was Porevit's turn to stay home. But the two elder brothers were no better for the lessons of the first two days and strode out arrogantly, wearing haughty smiles.

"What good could beauty be in hunting?" they mocked Porevit as they left.

Meanwhile Veles went to see the woodland demon, Lesovik, the Lord of the Woods, who grazed the herds of red deer. Lesovik was assisted in watching the herds of red deer by the woodland vile, playful nymphs who liked to play amorous games with the gods, but neither Rugievit or Porenut seemed particularly appealing to the woodland vile. For his plan, Veles then made himself into a regal stag with richly branching antlers, so large and beautiful that they would entice any hunter.

When the two brothers saw the herd, they noticed the majestic stag and were excited. Cautiously they crept up on the herd. But the stag was very skillful, hiding in the

*P*ORENUT *(Porenutius)—A deity whose name evokes the existence of Perun's cult throughout the Baltic region. The deity was represented with four faces and a fifth one on his chest. The deity's left hand touched the forehead and the right one touched the beard.*

herd and moving around so that only its beautiful antlers remained exposed, beckoning the hunters. Whenever the brothers thought they were close enough to deal a blow to the stag, it would smell them and lead the herd quickly away, deeper into the forest.

Rugievit and Porenut ran around the herd to stay down wind and hid, moving slowly and never taking their eyes off the stag. But they failed to notice that they were in the thick of the forest, surrounded by a giggling crowd of woodland vile, which was just what Veles and Lesovik had planned. Normally the woodland vile would have certainly been frightened and run at the sight of two such hunters but, because of the instructions of Lesovik,

they stayed, screaming and giggling. Embarrassed, gargantuan Rugievit and grisly Porenut could do nothing but stare at the alarm they had caused. Screaming and whooping, the woodland vile darted toward the herd and their protector, Lesovik. Naturally the red deer lost no time either and disappeared with the regal stag, far away into the thick of the forest.

Disappointed and ashamed, the two brothers headed for home empty-handed.

Veles was waiting for them at home, doubled over with laughter. At the sight of the unlucky hunters he managed to raise his head and nod to them. There was no need to say anything, the three brothers quickly guessed what their father had been doing.

Since that time the three have treated one another with greater respect and have learned to recognize each other's good qualities. They learned their lesson and know that they must work together to accomplish their goals.

Why
AUTUMN
Has No Patron God

Vesna and Morena the Pestilent are divine twins. Vesna, the goddess of spring, seduces Perun every year to signal the end of winter. Often naughty, she is known to romp and sing. She associates with the beautiful Lada, the goddess of love, spring, and youth, and Pizamar, the goddess of art and music. Their beauty, youth, and freshness are wonderful to look at and all of the gods take pleasure in beholding them.

The opposite of these three is the ugly Morena, the goddess of winter and death and the twin sister of Vesna. Only following anxious appeals did Svarozhich finally relent and command Mokosh the fertility goddess to allow the barren Morena to give birth to one, and only one, child. With Chernobog, the Black God, she conceived Triglav, who became known as a god of war. But now the grim and malevolent Morena at least occasionally softens her glance when her eyes fall on her son.

While these two goddesses rule over the winter and spring, it is Zhiva, the wife of Veles, who rules over the summer. Zhiva is the goddess of summer, crops, abundance, and plenitude, and is known to carry flowers and stalks of Veles' wheat. A summer flower is lasting, fragrant and useful, while a spring flower is often fragile, beaten by late snows and morning chills. An ear of wheat is the fulfillment of nature's labors. The farmer gains much more than mere subsistence from the summer, he gains meaning for his life. It was Zhiva who taught the people the art of cultivating the soil, of plowing it, and of sowing and harvesting crops. It was also on her advice that people began to store part of their grains for the next year, and it was Zhiva who showed farmers how to raise and graze cattle.

Morena guards the unfriendly but quiet winter, Vesna rules over the awakening spring, and Zhiva is entrusted with the warm and admired summer, season of bountiful harvests and blooms. But there is no patron of the autumn.

Stribog, the god of wind, had fallen in love with Chors, the goddess of the moon. But Stribog knew that Chors favored Radhost, one of the superior deities. So as to gain her affection, Stribog stole Radhost's beautiful black cloak scattered with silver and golden stars. The stars are laid out on it in various patterns so that each of them can quickly find its place on the nocturnal sky. Chors was wandering around the nocturnal countryside to keep an eye on her favorite little boy, Moon, or Mesiats, to make sure he was safe and sound. Just before dawn, when Chors was falling asleep after the long night, Stribog, enveloped in Radhost's black cloak, entered her room, and they conceived a girl.

The divine Radhost fumed and raged. It wasn't that Radhost particularly cared for Chors or that he was upset with the device Stribog had resorted to for the sake of seducing the goddess of the moon. What angered Radhost was that Stribog had stolen his cloak. Radhost had searched in vain for it in the evening. His servant, the demon Svetlonos, was given a good thrashing for his negligence. The god consequently had to leave for his watch without the cloak, angry and cursing his inability to keep discipline. When he returned to the oak in the morning, he found the cloak thrown on his throne as though it had been there all the time. Soon after, the malicious gods who had amused themselves at his expense told Radhost how Stribog had seduced Chors.

Radhost approached Svarozhich on the matter, insisting that Stribog should be appropriately punished. Duped and humiliated, Chors was unhappy that Radhost was angrier about his starry cloak than about how she had been abused and disgraced by Stribog. What made her more miserable, however, was the fear she had of the destiny of her child fathered by the wind god. She knew the gods would support Radhost in this matter and that her child would not be allowed to be born.

STRIBOG—*The god of air, specifically controlling the wind. The paga⸺⸺⸺ is that this elem⸺ made to blow or⸺ arrest for the go⸺ ment of people.⸺ Russian epic of⸺ century,* Slovo ⸺ Igorevom (Wor⸺ Regiment), *refe⸺ winds blowing⸺ that beat again⸺ troops as "Strib⸺ children," or as⸺ raised by this a⸺*

So Chors went before Svarozhich and the rest of the gods to plead for the life of her child. "We already have a goddess of spring, Vesna. We also have a goddess of summer, Zhiva. Even brutal winter has its patron and mistress, Morena, who is known to rule with a firm hand, though with justice and fairness. Couldn't my daughter possibly be goddess of the stretch of time that does not belong to anyone? Neither to the goddess of summer, since the crops have been taken from the fields, nor to Morena, since Krachun, the master of the Winter Solstice, has not yet turned over the scepter to the goddess of winter."

"Then one day someone will get it into their head that we could have a god or goddess for a time span that is not really spring because the nights are still frosty! Or—why not?—also specially for the time preceding the crops when the nights are already warm and short? Nay, Chors," Svarozhich answered, dismissing her plea. Prove nodded to show his support and consent.

"O Svarozhich, I pray you, don't make me finish off my poor little daughter who is not yet born! Don't double my dismay. At least let me have her for a few days after she is born. You will not begrudge me a little joy, will you?" Chors implored.

The sorrowful Chors was weeping so bitterly that Svarozhich was at a loss for words.

"Poor Chors," said Prove, the god of justice and law. He cast a disapproving glance at Stribog. "But it cannot be helped. That is justice."

Chors sobbed softly as her eyes went from one stone-faced deity to another. Some of the gods did not take any pity on her at all, while at least a few seemed to have some compassion for her. But all they could do was wait for Svarozhich to speak. Svarozhich felt sorry for Chors, but on the other hand, he could not help but enjoy the treacherous stratagem employed by Stribog. Yet the humiliation of the divine lord Radhost, should his grievance be neglected and the claim not enforced, might gnaw at the grandeur of Svarozhich himself. Radhost was entitled to substitute for Svarozhich in the evening side of the world. Moreover, as ruler of one of the quarters of the world, Radhost had

ZHIVA (Siva)—A goddess worshipped by the Polabians, a tribe once settled in what is now Germany. She must originally have been the embodiment of fecundity. This has been confirmed by the discovery that the goddess' name must have been "Zhiva," which is Slovak for "alive." This matches her role as responsible, like the East-Slavic Mokosh, for all the energies of life.

the prerogative of assuming the guise of Svarozhich and receive honors from people and demons on his behalf.

But then a lucky thought occurred to Svarozhich. He yielded not to the heart-wrenching entreaties of the abused woman. As soon as the child was born he took her in his hands, looked at her with his divine eye and proclaimed, "The child of the god Stribog and the goddess Chors exists not. It is just a dream."

Immediately the child vanished, leaving his hands empty and throwing Chors into the utmost despair. Svarozhich neither cursed the child nor sent its divine soul to Veles, ruler of the underworld. Svarozhich simply let the girl disappear like a fleeting dream. The poor wretch Chors continues to search the night sky for her lost child, which even as a dream has left her with memories.

"It is just a dream," repeated Svarozhich, and therefore the goddess never received a name. Unlike her, the dreamy and nostalgic season she was to patronize was not left anonymous. The season was called 'Yesen,' or Autumn, coming from 'sen,' a dream.

So no one rules over autumn, and Vesna and Morena have competing claims over autumn days. When the day is sunny and clear with enough light and warmth, the scepter is in the hands of Zhiva. When it rains or drizzles, when the weather is gloomy, cold, windy or foggy, and the remaining patches of green are tipped with white frost, the scepter has been taken away from her by Morena.

The people naturally prefer the life-enhancing Zhiva and make sacrificial offerings to her by pouring hemp oil on the ground and digging crumbs of food into the ground. They do this especially at the Winter Solstice, which is Krachun's festival, to convey to her the hopes they place upon her. Mid-summer, however, is the best time for paying her tribute, and people weave rings of flowers and march up to the hilltop shrines to leave these colorful rings as prayers to Zhiva, swearing by her name. But it is a binding vow, and if it is broken, Zhiva may release Nedostatok, Scarcity and Shortage, or the beastly Hlad, Hunger, from their tightly guarded dens to remind people of their vows.

Chors—An elemental character, specifically a moon deity, which in ancient Slavic lore is closely linked with the sun god Dazhbog (early peoples often thought that the Sun and the Moon were brother and sister) and embodies the unity between the two. The Moon was also conceived of as the eternal abode for souls. A fairly enigmatic inhabitant of the Slavonic pantheon, specifically that of Kievan Rus, the deity is mentioned in Russian chronicles.

Of
MORENA
and the Kingdom of Souls

The name of Morena is chanted during the Festival of Carrying Out Death. This is the ceremony where the ill-omened figure of the Grim Reaper is carried out beyond the bounds of the village and flung into the stream to celebrate the arrival of spring. The festival glorifies the end of the dominance of Winter with its gloom, desolation, and frequent sickness. The observance of the ceremony was considered a safeguard against pestilence and poor crops in the coming year.

At the moment when Perun hurls down lightning to free his hands to embrace the goddess of spring, Vesna, Morena the Pestilent leaves for the underworld kingdom of Veles. She has her own chambers in the underworld, including a damp cave with the palmprints of every mortal pressed into the walls to keep track of their lives and their time to die. Only her son Triglav, the gloomy and calculating god of war and husbandry, is ever allowed to enter Morena's chambers. With the end of the season of winter, she calls in the demon Death to submit her account book, to check the number of palmprints of departed souls.

The entrance to the kingdom of Veles is guarded by Mokosits. He guards the gate, as well as grazes the herds and watches the crops of Veles. And ever since a man called Slav plucked three dozen ears of wheat and the people began growing grain, Mokosits has had an assistant in the form of a three-headed wolf. The beast will assail and devour all who try to approach Veles' field, meadow, or herd. There is a narrow path between the field and the meadow that Death travels, bringing over the souls of departed mortals. The souls can no longer hear or see as they did when they were alive, they feel nothing, and even their fondest memories are gone. Lead by Death, they arrive in the realm of eternal rest docile and utterly helpless. The narrow path takes them to a gangplank spanning the edges of such a profound abyss that the bottom cannot be seen. Deep in the bottom of the abyss runs a river of tears shed by the souls that have been left forever in Nav.

Veles' kingdom consists of two territories, Raj and Nav. Nav holds the souls that have earned eternal suffering. Those souls are kept in black dungeons where not a single ray of sunlight or sound or even fragrance can penetrate. The souls must wait and wait, hoping that the Fates will eventually show them mercy and release them to Raj. Occasionally these souls are forced to take the shape of ravens and black crows to go punish the living for not duly honoring the dead or for neglecting the graves of the dead. But Nav is carefully guarded by Morena and Death, and not a single soul can ever escape from them.

Raj does not need to be guarded. The territory of Raj is a meadow full of light, birds, and flowers, as well as songs, with a large lake in the center. This is the place for entertaining souls, where the dead are almost as happy as the gods themselves in the Giant Oak. Raj does need to be guarded, since the souls there do not remember their former lives. There is nothing to call them away, since they have no memory of their loved ones, friends, or even foes, that would tempt them.

A short while after birth, Morena and Death arrange for the making of each mortal's palmprint on the wall of the cave. On the same wall, beside each palmprint, they hang a sooty smoking lamp, one for each person. No one is privileged to look inside and see the bottom, so that no one has any way to learn how much oil is left to keep his or her lamp burning. Death alone is given the right to stick its long and bony finger into the lamps, and only Death knows how much time is left for every living person.

The immortal gods have always had their favorites among the mortals. Pizamar, the goddess of art and music, had herself once been a mortal, and was enchanted with the singing of mortals. One in particular, the youthful Igric the Wandering Minstrel, caught her ear and eye with his masterfully chanted verses. Igric was the son of a wealthy Slavic lord, but instead of turning to the sword and the lance as his father wanted, Igric took to singing and poetry and composing verses and songs. Igric's father was annoyed with his son's disinterest in the triumphs of war. As the first-born male, Igric was heir to his father's wealth and obliged by custom to be a warrior. Pizamar, an enthusiastic singer herself, would sit on the banks of the river near the seven towns of Nitrava. There she would hide behind the branches of the willow trees, where she could listen to the beautiful voice of the young Igric. Sometimes Pizamar would sing the songs of the young man, and eventually she fell in love with him.

This did not escape the eye of Svarozhich. When Pizamar had merely flirted with the mortal, Svarozhich had simply smiled. And since she had become a goddess, Svarozhich had lost all interest in her. But as soon as he discerned the flames of love and desire in her eyes, the sting of wounded pride prompted him to call for Veles.

"Tell Death that she should stick her finger into the young man's lamp," Svarozhich commanded, pointing to Igric.

"Should she pour a little out as well?" joked Veles. He had noticed some time ago that Pizamar, disguised as a shepherdess, often talked with Igric, and knew that the lord of the gods would not tolerate the situation for long.

After Veles had reported back to Svarozhich, Svarozhich could not resist the desire to torment Pizamar a little.

"So you have taken a liking to this young singer, haven't you?" he said to her, making sure to sound indifferent. "I wonder if you know his days are numbered. Death is getting ready to bring him to Veles."

Pizamar was seized with grief and refused to answer Svarozhich. Remembering well the reason for her own immortality, she ran away, cursing him under her breath.

The more profound her sadness grew, the more often Pizamar would go to meet with Igric. Hard though he tried, nothing Igric could do could comfort Pizamar, as a lasting sorrow had taken hold of her heart.

Eventually the inconsolable goddess made up her mind to take a desperate step. She had no doubt that Svarozhich had spoken the truth about the short time left for Igric, but she decided to try to prolong her happiness with the young man as much as possible. First, she gave Igric an earthenware tablet to get his palmprint. Then the resourceful Pizamar approached Mokosh. The goddess of fertility took pity on the desperate woman in love and helped her by making a special gown that would allow Pizamar to creep into the underworld unnoticed. The gown was carefully made so that Mokosits would recognize the handiwork of his mother and allow the wearer to pass. Now wearing the gown, Pizamar took the tablet of the palmprint and slipped into the underworld, into the dank cave of Morena. At last, she managed to find the palmprint of Igric and filled up his lamp.

But on the way out of the underworld, Pizamar was caught by the three-headed wolf. Somehow the gods were not particularly upset about such a breach of the divine law. They did agree with Veles, however, that Pizamar had to be punished. Svarozhich knew that his punishment would be lenient, but even so, neither Veles nor Morena pressed for a harsher judgment.

Igric lived for many more years, but never again did he catch sight of the beautiful young shepherdess. Svarozhich's verdict was that Pizamar could not assume any guise the human eye could perceive, and she was forbidden from uttering any sound the human ear could hear whenever she was in the presence of Igric. This was a terrible pity, since divine Pizamar would often sit by his side as he sang, and the mournful Igric knew nothing of it. Only the gods could see that Pizamar sat beside him and cried.

It had been the duty of Death to guard the lamps of the mortals, but from time to time she had to leave the lamps unattended when she went to fetch the souls of the departed to bring them to the underworld. In the meantime the crafty gods would slip in and fill up the lamps of their favorites. To put an end to this practice, Svarozhich finally gave Death an enormous bat with seven hundred and seventy-seven eyes to guard the lamps at all times. A single glance from one eye of this bat burns through any garment, allowing Veles to immediately recognize the intruder and demand punishment. To make sure that the gods properly respected and feared the bat, Svarozhich demonstrated the power of its gaze by allowing it to burn a hole right through his own majestic garment.

From time to time Veles still can be persuaded to release a soul from Raj into the world of the living, but Morena is uncompromising when it comes to the souls from Nav. She believes that they have to repent for their failure to heed the commands of the gods and that order can only be kept in the world through strict enforcement of the rules of the gods.

How the
STONE AGE
Came to an End

PERUN (Pyerun, Perkonis, Perkons, Perkunas, or Perkuns)—As the counterpart of Zeus and Jupiter, he is the divinity of the thunderstorm and lightning. His worship appears to have been shared by all Aryans. In Old Russia he was revered as the highest god, presiding over the Slavic pantheon. Oaks were sacred to him. He is the ancient Indo-European thunder god dating back to the period of the "expansion" of Indo-European tribes. Perun in his extended capacity was regarded as the harvest-giver. Perun was also appealed to as the great fertilizing power, as raging thunderstorms with heavy rains caused the earth to bear fruit. His usual attribute, a

What Perun could really not stand was the inconsistency of human nature. He had been the first, following Svarozhich, to whom the people had started to bow down, which was the right thing to do, since he wielded thunder and lightning, as well as rain. In the spring his thunderbolts would stir the air and awaken new life. But his time of unshared worship had gone, as the people became too sure of the onset of spring each year. They began to pray equally to the other gods and worshipped Perun more out of politeness than humility. So Perun thought about how he might remind the people that he was truly more important than the other gods.

The neglected deity looked for an opportune day for carrying out his scheme. Perun hurled down his lightning forks and thunderbolts, igniting trees, dry shrubs, field grass, lush pines, and massive oaks. The mountain heights everywhere were ablaze, ignited by the fire which had flashed down from the heavens. Even the thriving valleys began to catch fire and burn up.

But there was more to fire than its destructive power. And discovering this other side, the side so jealously guarded by the gods, Perun was well aware, would help the treacherous race of people. Fire could become the source of endless benefits and power that could work miracles. Its scorching heat could make rocks sweat and release hot trickles of copper and iron from their ore seams. To prevent people from getting these gifts, Perun, after setting fire to the earth, would summon the whole crew of demons. Wind demons, the obedient servants of the god Stribog, headed by their lord Oblachnik the Cloud-Bringer, started shedding drops of rain on the earth. They puffed up their cheeks and put out every tongue of flame, even the smallest one. They kept blowing until there was not even a trace of glowing embers or smoke on the earth. People could not help but notice the power of fire to eat everything, alive or dead, in its path. They watched with their own eyes as clay, when heated enough, turned to stone. Perun had made sure that people knew the pain fire could bring and so were afraid of it, and it was this fear that had kept them from learning the benefits of this elemental force.

But in pursuit of his design, Perun picked a sacred oak grove with a young oak tree growing at the center. This sanctuary was fenced-in in honor of Perun himself, and was the same one that had once been watched over by Mokosits. Aiming exactly at the young tree in the center, Perun sent one small lightning fork into its tender young crown. The tree immediately caught fire and started blazing. The greedy flames bickered and snapped as they devoured the less juicy leaves. The frightened priests were in a panic, screaming with fear and turning to run away. The men had no doubt that the fire was a bad omen from their patron god, Perun, and began speculating about the reason for the god's wrath, but this only exacerbated their terror.

Perun did not keep them waiting long. He made his divine response, sending his voice right into the midst of the raging fire. He addressed the scared priests.

"Just warm your cold hands over Perun's hearth fire. A small fire will be your good servant if you keep it kindling with dry wood."

But Perun's priests didn't understand the counsel correctly, and were so afraid of the flames that they kept their distance, allowing the fire to go out.

Perun grabbed another bolt of lightning and hurled it down, this time at a larger tree. It, too, immediately caught fire. As terrified as they were, this time the priests did not flee and listened to Perun's command.

"Just warm your cold hands over Perun's hearth fire. A small fire will be your good servant if kindled with dry tree branches."

battle-axe, was a favorite weapon of Slavic warriors. According to Nestor's chronicle (by a learned monk of the Pechora Monastery in Kiev) "Povest' vremennykh liet" (Primary Chronicle) of the early twelfth century, the Slavs, who believed Perun to be the lord of all things, kept perpetual fires in his honor and sacrificed in Kiev every kind of victim to him, including humans. Oxen were however the most common sacrificial victims. The custom survived well into the Christian Era. In Bulgaria, for example, an ox or cow was slain on the feast of St. Il'ya (the Russian name for the Old Testament prophet Eliajah/Elijah, who, following the adoption of Christianity by Russia, replaced the thunder god Perun). A feast was commonly held. On these occasions people assembled in great multitudes. They ate and drank and called upon Perun. For a long time he was secretly worshipped in what is now Slovakia, though official Christian rites and festivals had already been established and enforced. This is supported by the finding of Perun's idol in Bratislava. The Christian Church sensitively but steadily undermined Perun's cult by transferring many of his powers and attributes to the prophet Il'ya (such as that of being able to call down rain and fire from heaven).

This time the priests understood what the god was telling them, but they were still scared out of their wits. Plucking up their courage, they made themselves stay and, heeding Perun's counsel, inched their way closer to the fire. Keeping a respectful distance, they did not feel any painful burning, but rather, a blessing of warmth. The priests stretched their hands toward the fire, palms downward, enjoying the pleasant warmth emanating from the flames. Yet they did not follow the second part of Perun's command and failed to add any dry branches to the fire. Again it went out.

Perun looked around to see the reaction of his divine peers. He was loath to annoy them when it came to the sensitive matters of prestige and status. Luckily, no one seemed to have noticed his endeavors. Heartened, the god dropped another bolt of lightning from his stout hand. A third oak, a magnificent giant, crackled in the fire. Once more Perun appealed to the priestly attendants of his oak grove. This time the priests listened very carefully and understood everything he said, and he finally managed to soothe their fears.

"Ye, my faithful servants! Do make your cold hands warm at Perun's hearth fire," he launched into a loud harangue. "Give me a patient hearing. A small fire will be your good servant if fed with dry wood. Don't be scared of drawing closer to it. I promise it won't hurt you!"

That was when Stribog heard him speak. Stribog was about to drive a storm cloud over to the fire and whistle for Oblachnik when Perun rushed over and covered Stribog's mouth.

"Leave it as it is," Perun said, trying to persuade Stribog. "It's just a small fire doomed to go out as so many before it have. You see, my quiver is full of holes, therefore I must have lost some of my fiery arrows. . . Why make so much fuss about nothing?"

Stribog granted Perun's request. He could see that it really was only a small fire and not really worth bothering about. Besides, he had had a busy day and was drowsy, so he didn't feel like doing anything at the moment anyway. He was more than happy to assent and leave the entire

Slavic pagan shrines— Everything we know of these comes from written testimonies and archeological excavations. Unique among the latter are the sites of several quite remarkable sanctuaries. A temple within the castle-fortress known as Radegast (Riedigost) was apparently an ornate wooden construction. For protection it rested on animal horns driven into the foundation. The shrine was adorned with woodcarvings of gods and goddesses as well as wooden statues in the full panoply of armor. The temple on the

thing alone. But by this time the priests had put some dry twigs on the fire as Perun had told them. Sparks flew up, and the fed fire did not die out. Meanwhile Perun, hidden in the very midst of the flames, kept whispering to the priests.

"Get a move on and keep adding more sticks and logs!"

As the fire continued to burn, the other gods finally

Arkon featured a richly painted and carved wooden fence which at the same time roofed another construction. It appears to have been dominated by a wooden statue of superhuman size, featuring four heads. Heathen temples commonly housed tribal treasuries or even those of whole tribal unions. In Gross Raden near Schwerin-Zverin (Germany), there was an extensive construction with 53 statues made of oak nearby. This construction, situated on the edge of a settlement at the foot of a

hill-fort, also served as a public meeting place. A sacrificial site unearthed within Castle Bogit in Galich, Galicia (Ukraine) appears to have featured an idol of the river Zbrucz in the middle. A circular cultic site has also been discovered at Pohansko near Breclav (Moravia, Czech Republic). More heathen sanctuaries have been excavated next to the princely palace in Kiev and Novgorod. Sacred woodland glades also served for heathen worship, one being, for example, that near Oldenburg in Wagria, where

a sanctuary dedicated to the god Prove was maintained up to the Middle Ages. The sacred space was enclosed with a finely decorated wooden fence, whose two magnificent gates would only let in those who were coming to make offerings on the altar of their god. The Slavs were known to honor not only groves, but also trees and water sources. A tiny rain-water stream in Stara Kourim, the Czech Republic, used to form a little lake. The ancient Slavs surrounded the reservoir with a mound and would kindle

began to take notice. The serenity of the Giant Oak was broken as the gods began quarreling, reproaching each other with old sins. There seemed to be no end to the general mistrust and accusations.

Svarozhich was beside himself with rage. Perun tried to make excuses, blaming the whole thing on the holes in his quiver. Stribog watched Perun suspiciously but chose to remain silent. He felt guilty for his laziness and thought that Svarozhich might punish him as well.

While this was going on, Perun's obedient priests were doing their best to keep the fire going. They continued to gather dry leaves and dry tree branches and started to keep a pile in reserve. One of them raced off to summon whole clans for a thanksgiving ceremony dedicated to Perun as the god who had granted them the most precious gift of all. Overnight people ceased to be afraid of formerly abhorred natural forces. The unveiling of the mystery of fire made them feel stronger and safer than ever before. People rejoiced, overwhelmed by the same passions and expectations that the fire had aroused in the priests.

In the Giant Oak the noise and arguments wouldn't end. Even the key culprit, Perun, was frowning in earnest, although he felt a certain measure of pride at being the celestial patron of fire. But he couldn't show that yet, as it would upset Svarozhich even more than the ceaseless arguments among the gods. Like angry wasps the gods went on attacking each other, loudly exchanging insults. Prove was just about to pronounce his judgment when Svarozhich raised his hand.

This gesture put an end to the bickering, and not one god even dared to murmur.

"I pronounce the advent of this Era's third stage," Svarozhich said solemnly. "This is the last stage of our Era. The gift of fire bestowed upon the people has ended the Stone Age and begun the Iron Age."

ritual fires within the enclosed sanctuary. Many shrines and cult precincts were dedicated to minor divinities—demons as well as stream- and tree-spirits, this sort of worship being well attested for all the great European families of Aryan stock. Very often such sanctuaries consisted merely of an earth pile or a clearing in an ocean of greenery, with either a pole or a wooden idol set up in the middle. The hallowed spots were commonly surrounded by a round trench.

CHAPTER 3

The Iron Age

Under the
FAVOR OF THE GODS

It did not take people long to learn that the fire which the gods had tamed and given them provided not only light and warmth, but also protection against wolves and other dangerous beasts. Nor did the people fail to realize that the clay beneath their hearths hardened into warm rock and the seams in this rock squeezed out red-hot trickles of the metal that came to be known as iron. Tools forged from this and other metals were finer and more efficient than any the people had ever been able to make from stone or bone, and time proved that Perun's gift of fire was the greatest gift any god had ever given the people. With fire and iron, however, came new technologies that could be applied to tilling, mining, and hunting, but also to warfare, a very ambiguous development in human affairs.

The gods of war being so many, it did not take long to find out that fire could help destroy things as easily as it could help create them. Mere masculine prowess and feats of strength were not equal to the new level of destructive capability. Before long, people discovered how to use fire to destroy life, to burn entire villages to the ground, and to shoot fire-tipped arrows into the camps of their enemies. With this new power came the desire not only to herd animals or plant seeds but also to exert power over other groups of humans. The heart-wrenching sight of settlements reduced to smoldering ashes and rows of graves encouraged people to erect stone walls and stone shrines to the gods.

The large group of war gods, including Perun, Svantovit, Triglav, the three divine brothers, Yarovit, and Chernobog, as well as the demon-giants Ashliks and Bazilisk, had done their best to ensure that the secrets they had given away to people were used to promote the art of war. As a result, people began to measure divine favor by successes in robbery, pillaging, and destruction. The war gods were truly pleased to see the destructive forces in motion and were happy that their gifts were used in this way. But other gods were happiest when the divine gifts were applied to everyday life, and still others were overjoyed when some people began to create beautiful objects and recognized them as works of art.

It was a time of great changes. People were tilling the soil with a plow instead of the digging stick or hoe. They learned how to forge sharp swords and iron tips for their long spears, and they wore metal helmets and carried heavy metal shields in battle.

But now that people needed a lot of metal, they found that they were permanently short of the precious ore.

They had gathered all they could find on the ground and began grumbling and complaining about the shortage. The people dug feverishly into the places where they used to pick up iron ore and unearthed more and more. After they had collected all of these metal-bearing lumps, the most daring among them broke up the stones in search of still more. Eager to reach ore seams, they did not even pause before hammering and shattering cliffs.

And suddenly the seams were all gone.

"Do not dare beat the Earth, or she will refuse to give you your bread!" the elders had warned, but to no avail. Now that the seams were gone, the elders again offered counsel, promising that the gods would punish them more severely than by merely taking away the iron ore if the digging continued.

"Repent your sins and make sacrifices to the goddesses Pripelaga, Mokosh, and Zhiva!" pressed the priests. "And make sure it is the costliest sacrifice of all—a man!"

Quite a few of them took these words to heart and started considering the counsel of the priests in earnest. They even talked to the most valiant warriors, trying to persuade them to go to the very edge of the world, where the Nemtsi-Germans lived, to capture one of the Germans to use to placate the gods.

"Let us placate Pripelaga first of all," they agreed, "for none other than she has scattered the lumps of bountiful treasure all over the earth."

"Kovlad, the Iron Lord and ruler of caves, is equally important," added the miners, who had the job of digging into the earth for the precious ores.

"Forget not his wife, Runa, and their servants, Permoniks and kobolds," reminded the wives and children.

"O wisest! Do you really think this would be the right thing to do?" ventured a young priest trying to stop the elders. "Let us try to regain the favor of the gods by the power of words, not by the violence of blood."

"Words?" shouted the people distrustfully.

"With words!" sniffed the warriors.

"By words?" the elders asked, horrified. They had lived longer than the others and knew the limitations of words.

"Verily, by words," confirmed the young priest quietly. "Tonight there will be a full moon. By the time of the next full moon I will have returned and brought the god's mercy. I am going to pray for this to the gods," he told the solemn assembly before asking the elders to let him leave the hamlet.

The council of elders gave their consent but, to be on the safe side, they ordered the warriors to get ready for a long journey as well.

"And be sure to take the mistletoe along to protect you," they advised the warriors.

While the priest set off for the mountains, the armed warriors marched over to the very edge of their kingdom in search of a few Nemtsi-Germans they could capture and take back for sacrifices to the gods.

Determined to find Kovlad at all costs, the young priest wandered in through the mountains, combing cave after cave in search of the Iron-Keeper. All this effort was in vain, and no matter how hard the priest searched he could not find the god. Anxiously he watched as the crescent face of the moon grew leaner and leaner.

The moon's face started putting on flesh, the signal that he would have to start heading back to the village to reach it before the moon grew full as he had promised. He was losing hope and almost lost his way in one of the tortuous caves on his perilous way home. Disheartened and exhausted, he finally fell asleep in a cave. While he slept he had a dream, and in that dream an unknown force lifted him up and he was bathed in a dazzling light. A voice spoke from the middle of the light, and it was the voice of Kovlad himself.

"You have to appease Pripelaga, the great goddess of the earth, and she will withdraw her divine command to hide from people for good all the gold, silver, copper, and iron ores. Tell your people to abandon digging for the metal-bearing ores and rather care for Mother Earth. Till the soil. It holds something much more precious than all the gold that lies spellbound inside the rocks. Sacrifice a chamois to Pripelaga. You will find one with a broken leg lying outside the cave."

The young priest then awoke, feeling pleased that he remembered the dream so clearly. He left the cave and found the injured chamois lying right where Kovlad had promised. Hoisting the animal over he shoulder, he started for home, repeating the words of the dream over and over to himself. The young priest hurried as much as he could, as the sun was setting and the full moon was already in the sky.

The hamlet seemed deserted when he reached it, as all the people were gathered at the sacrificial site just beyond the village. The warriors had returned before him, dragging along a few helpless captives. The priests of the sacred groves, caves, and shrines were all there, eager to offer the sacrifices to Pripelaga. The young priest ran up the hill to the altar to relate his experiences to the people.

"Yes, the elders were right!" he shouted at the top of his lungs. "Do not dare beat the Earth, or she will not yield any crops and leave us without bread. Care for her and she will reward us with her fruit. Release them from their chains," he commanded, pointing at the prisoners. "Let us make them servants of this sanctuary. You shall not offend the Great Mother Earth with their blood. Let us appease her with this sacrifice!" On saying this, he killed the chamois.

The people gasped as the blood gushed out onto the altar. The priest bowed low, then knelt and kissed the earth.

After that the elder priests brought forward seven sacrificial bulls, seven measures of corn, and seven barrels of mead to the altar. Seven priests washed their faces and drank the fresh blood. They loudly chanted seven invocations, hoping that they would reach the ears of not only Pripelaga but also the goddesses Mokosh and Zhiva.

The night under the full moon was very long. The first rays of morning sun were in the sky by the time the worshippers had performed the last ritual dance and left, exhausted, to sleep their short sleep drowned in mead.

Pripelaga's divine heart melted. She had appreciated the sacrifice made on her altar and the festival held in her honor, and she benignly listened to the supplications of the priests. From that day people could again mine for ore in the rocks, and the gods no longer felt the digging to be an offense to the Great Mother Earth.

How
RADHOST
Descended to the Earth

The god Radhost, despite his sinister reputation as lord of the evening side of the world, has always been known as one to enjoy a good festival. Whenever he happened to hear about the news of someone's death, or a wedding ceremony, or the birth of a child, he wouldn't hesitate to attend in one of his favorite guises as a traveling minstrel, soothsayer, or wizard. Telling fortunes or conjuring tricks were relatively easy things for a god, and Radhost was also an exception singer, performing carefree ballads of unbridled happiness. He always had a fine time, sipping mead and rye beer, even though the drinks did not taste nearly as good as the drink in the Giant Oak.

Whenever Radhost took a liking to the village and the people hosting him, he would reward the hospitable community with an unexpected gift. On one occasion in early times, when the lean year with its failed crops had made food scarce, Radhost joined one Slavic clan at their table. Despite the scarcity, they honored the traveler who had found his way to their hearth in the best possible way.

This plain community allowed Radhost, disguised as a weary traveler, to join them at their table for a meal. However, the people of this village understood that all travelers have a reason for journeying and wandering, and thought it unbecoming and even uncivil to ask the traveler for his reason for leaving his home. They followed this considerate rule of hospitality, well aware that the man could easily have lost his name and home and had set out in the world to find it anew.

But one of the men at the table was old and recognized as having grown a little senile. He asked the traveler, "Where have you come from and where are you heading?"

93

RADHOST (Radegast, Radogost, Riadogost, Rugavit)—A deity with attributes and characteristics similar to Svantovit. Early chroniclers, such as the Danish chronicler Saxo Grammaticus, are the only sources to mention this divinity. Along with Svarog, Radhost was among the first gods the Slavonic people inhabiting the Baltic coastal districts referred to by name. This deity is linked with Castle Radegost and the surviving description of its sanctuary by the chronicler Thietmar includes the cult. Radhost appears to have been initially a personal name, and research into its provenience suggests that it might have signified the one "who is really welcome as a guest." As a native name, it still lingers in Germany, the Czech Republic (especially Moravia), and Lower Austria. Traces of the original function of Radhost-Svarozhich as the tribal deity of the Retharii in Rethra (now in Germany) have endured in the widespread cultural presence in this territory of one-time cult animals such as the horse and the boar.

The god Radhost, in his guise of a wandering minstrel, smiled and strummed a tune to avoid a direct reply, and asked, "Shall I sing?" The god struck up a song about the benevolent gods who care for their human flocks and are intimately familiar with their concerns and cares. Not only do the gods know about the troubles of the world, but they would also come to the aid of the people who were kind-hearted and obedient.

"Will they indeed help? Are you sure of it?" the obtrusive old man asked after the song. "Could you tell us when the gods help people in need?"

The other guests at the table also joked and laughed, encouraged by the mead and not really thinking about the inappropriate questions the old man was asking, questions that could easily insult the gods. The wandering minstrel simply joined in the laughter and merriment, singing at the poor table as if it were a princely one.

In the morning, once their hangover had gone, the previous night's revelers stumbled upon a dozen fat oxen tethered to the outer gate of their walled village. Nobody claimed ownership and the people of the town were at a loss as to what to do with the oxen. Finally, they decided to take the oxen to the local temple, where the priests placed them in a pasture adjacent to the one for their sacred boar. After three days, no merchant or cowherd had come to claim the cattle, so the temple oracle communicated with the gods, and the sacred boar gave the omen that the oxen had been donated by one of the gods. In gratitude they immediately slew one of the oxen, offering its warm blood, hide, and bones as a sacrifice to the generous god. They then feasted on the animal and repeated this every month for the entire year. All of this took place in Rethra, where the people have never forgotten the great god Radhost.

And when Radhost liked an entire settlement, he would present it with an even more unexpected gift, such as he had given to settlers on Rugen Island. This was a community that had always shown Radhost respect, but he had felt the need to put their faith to a test.

At that time there were false prophets wandering all over the countryside preaching and promoting faith in strange foreign gods, blaspheming against the old gods of the land and trying to separate the people from their old gods. Sadly, some people lent these prophets an ear.

The divine Radhost, his face and clothes changed entirely, entered one community and began to preach and invoke the new gods. A crowd of curious onlookers gathered around him in the marketplace. There were not many merchants, as in those times merchants spent much more time traveling than anything else. The townspeople came for a time, then drifted away, dismissing the prophet as a madman, as they usually did. A few, however, lingered, and Radhost went on trying to sway them with his tales of the new gods. He spoke eloquently, even more so than the priest who went yearly to the same village to speak on behalf of Radhost himself.

After a time Radhost became convinced that he had failed to convert any of the listeners that remained. Even a god does not lack vanity, and Radhost was overjoyed, but not entirely convinced, that no one had failed the difficult test. So he worked a miracle right in front of them, throwing his left arm up in the air and making a falcon fly out of his sleeve and hover above the heads of the crowd. He made the same motion with his right arm and a wild dove flew out.

"Now behold how my god will save the dove!" declared Radhost in the same manner as the false prophets. They watched, and the dove flew away into the clouds without having been attacked by the falcon.

"This time, behold, I am not going to supplicate my god for its protection," he said as he waved his right arm again and made a second dove appear. As soon as the second dove began to beat its wings, the falcon swooped down to catch the bird in its talons right above the heads of the crowd. The people gave an approving scream. Radhost, playing his part as a prophet, called upon the people to renounce their feeble gods. But the people hesitated.

"Well, plead with them then to save this dove!" he mocked the small crowd, once more waving his arm. A third dove soared up above the marketplace. "The falcon's hunger has been appeased, therefore the task your gods are challenged with is fairly easy to perform."

The falcon again swooped on the dove and the poor bird found itself caught in the talons.

"So what?" he shouted at the crowd.

At first they kept silent. Then they all began talking at once, until finally they chose someone to speak for them. The man stepped forward and proceeded to tell the prophet how their esteemed and loved god Radhost protected their village from enemies, and how when they needed his help they would eagerly pray and Radhost would give them his divine help.

"And it may well be that your god will heed your invocations as his prophet and work miracles for you," the man continued. "Yet we don't know your god, therefore we cannot simply begin worshipping him. We feel that it would be best if you left, and took your god along with you."

Radhost was overwhelmed with deep gratitude for such staunch faith in him, and, were he not a god, the words would have squeezed tears from his eyes. And the reward he gave was more than regal. When the guardian priest of the sacred fire awoke the next morning, there beside the altar was a warrior's suit of armor, sparkling like the Sun and the Moon and all the stars taken together. The beautifully decorated armor was interpreted by the priests and soothsayers as an omen of Radhost's favor, as well as his commitment to their protection. Warriors that had survived the great wars and battles came to view the armor and recognized it as that worn by Radhost when he had ridden at their side in those wars. And all marveled at how not a single man could lift so much as the helmet, which was not surprising considering it was the armor of a god.

And Radhost was not the only god who felt comfortable in his own temples with the people who paid him tribute. Stribog enjoyed visiting Moravia, Triglav would go often to Stettin, Perun favored Kiev, Svantovit traveled to Arcona when he could, and Svarozhich divided his love equally between Nitra and Devin. And as for the merry Yarilo, he would wander over half the world at the time of the harvest.

THE BIRD SIMARGL
and the Rainbow

SIMARGL—A mysterious divinity of the eastern Slavs. It was included in Prince Vladimir's Kievan pantheon established in 980 and described by Nestor in his chronicle "Povest' vremennykh liet" (Primary Chronicle). Another source, "Slovo nekojego christol'uba" (A Word of a Certain Christian Worshipper), refers in this context to two gods, Sim and Rygl. This deity had a dual nature, actually being twins, which goes well with the old Indo-European perception throughout the mythological lore of such peoples as the Indians, the Iranians, the Getae, the Greeks, and the Romans. A wooden idol, representing a two-headed god and found by archaeologists on the so-called Fishman's Island (Fisherinsel), near Neubrandenburg (now Germany), is proof of the historical existence of this cult.

The new skills, crafts, and occupations that had been created by the emerging cities changed the lives of people beyond recognition. There was new joy expressed in art, music, song, and the resplendent colors of festal attire and city structures that enchanted even the gods. The gods took special pleasure in following the new activities of the people. Their divine curiosity observed not only the palaces and sacred temples, but also the lower orders in the cities, including the farmers, cobblers, shipbuilders, colliers, and fullers. And while the Giant Oak remained home to the gods, more and more of them spent greater spans of time away from the sacred tree.

For that reason the divine twins, Sim and Rygl, grew depressed. They always enjoyed the company of the other gods but, as they were joined to each other, they were not free to leave the branches of the oak as the other gods were. When they wanted to take a closer look at the world, they had to take the shape of a bizarre two-headed bird. When the gods Sim and Rygl changed into Simargl, the divine mother-bird, they fed and looked after the children of the gods. The goddess Simargl was known as a reliable, responsible, and caring wet-nurse who rarely left the Giant Oak, and then only when someone desperately needed her help and pleaded for it.

But for Sim and Rygl to fly away from the Giant Oak as Simargl, all they had to do was hold their hands and close their eyes. Then their shiny plumage would rustle and their brass beaks would snap open and closed. As a divine bird, Simargl cared deeply for all the feathered, the fur-covered, and even the scaly creatures of the world. Her sharp copper talons were known as the scourge of all those who hunted out of an obsession to kill and not simply out of the need for food.

When Simargl chased the zealous hunters and left bloody marks on their faces with her copper talons, the other gods would praise her. The twins felt flattered that the gods were holding them in such esteem, so that no sooner would they catch and punish some cruel poachers than they would race back to the Giant Oak to call on the other gods to admire their exploits.

The bird Simargl was very happy until she was asked to raise the three divine brothers, the darlings of the large family of the gods. The three brothers, Rugievit, Porenut, and Porevit, grew fond of playing mean tricks on Simargl as they got older. And the older they got, the crueler their pranks became. They vexed Simargl sorely and wouldn't give her a moment's peace. In vain, she implored their parents to take over their upbringing. But Veles and Zhiva would merely offer Simargl gifts and extract empty promises of better behavior from their unruly sons.

As the young gods grew to maturity, they were presented with the gifts that were to establish how they would be venerated as deities. Young Rugievit received a gold-headed spear, Porevit was given a bow strung with silver cord, and Porenut received a golden battle-axe very similar to the one carried by the god of thunder, Perun. Immediately the three brothers wanted to test these gifts, which were symbols of warfare and hunting prowess. But the rest of the gods threw a large feast and celebration in honor of the three brothers, accompanied by large amounts of mead.

As the feasting neared an end, the gods began to drift off into sleep among the branches of the Giant Oak. But not the three divine brothers. They had been anxiously waiting to test their new weapons, so they took advantage of the situation and went down to the earth. The woods and forests across the world were literally pierced by flying arrows and spears, and the heavy strokes of the battle-axe resounded throughout. From all over came the groans and roaring of badly injured and mutilated animals.

And up in the Giant Oak the gods still slept. Sim and Rygl were the first to awaken. Since no one else was awake, Simargl the divine bird stretched wide her wings and flew off to the morning side of the world. There her kind heart almost failed her. The air was heavy with the stench of fresh blood. Simargl looked and saw birds, fish, deer, bear, bison, boars, lynx, chamois and everything else that could still move terror-stricken and rushing headlong through the woods in flight. Never had the world seen such horror, and the brutality of the massacre brought tears to Simargl.

But her grief quickly turned to a rage that made her blood boil. She flapped her wings and soared high up into the sky. Straining her keen eyes, she surveyed the whole world, and there was not a single place where blood had not been shed. The entire earth was strewn with the carcasses of dead and dying animals.

"Who?" the horrified Simargl's two throats roared in unison. "Who? Who?" the wailing echo repeated. But Simargl, her eyes darting fiery beams, had already sighted the villains, and she could not believe it when she saw the bloodthirsty young gods committing such atrocities.

Furiously she attacked the three brothers, ripping and tearing at them with her copper talons and brass beaks. Outraged, she struck again and again. Vainly the three brothers pleaded for mercy and help, but their pitiful cries meant nothing to Simargl. In her rage she just kept delivering her terrible blows.

The noise and cries for help rudely shook the gods from their sleep. Hurriedly, they rushed to help the three brothers, but the gods could only manage to tear free the youngest, Porevit, from the talons of the furious bird. It took much longer to get Simargl to release Rugievit and Porenut, and the two older brothers were disfigured forever.

The parents of the brothers, Veles and Zhiva, went before the other gods. They complained about Simargl and begged Pereplut, the god of memory, to never erase from the memories of the gods what had happened to their children. They then turned to Prove, the god of justice, and demanded that Simargl be punished for her crime.

The highest god of all, Svarozhich, knew that the antics of the three brothers had been wrong, and that most of the other gods disapproved as well. So he appreciated Simargl's promptness in stopping the killing, as well as her speed and boldness, but at the same time he had to reprimand the sacred bird for her excessive zeal, because Veles and Zhiva had made a very strong plea. So Svarozhich declared that from that time on, Simargl's duties would be those of a herald, summoning the other gods to the Giant Oak. She would obey only the orders of Svarozhich or his deputy Svantovit. When the gods were summoned by Simargl, they were supposed to leave whatever they were doing and go immediately to the Giant Oak. In times of extreme emergency, Perun was also given the power to summon them with a mighty bolt of lightning or thunder, and he would urge on the slow with hail and heavy rain.

"Our Simargl, who is yonder, will give you directions and show you the way," added Svarozhich as he pointed to the bird, who sat on a branch with her beaks and claws shining ominously in the sun.

From then on, whenever there was lightning and thunder with rain or drizzle, and the gods were to hurry home to the Giant Oak, Simargl would fly across the sky, charting a path straight to the tree for gods all over the world to see. This path would be a rainbow, made up of the fine colors playing on the shiny beaks and claws of the bird Simargl, the messenger of the gods.

How PERUN defied SVAROZHICH

One morning the Slavs were distracted from their work by exceptionally worrisome news. A local youth had coming running into the village and breathlessly announced that the water of the sacred lake had turned red. Everyone leapt to their feet. Suddenly a great roaring noise resounded throughout the valley, and the people could feel the ground tremble beneath their feet.

It was the boar! The prophetic boar, kept by the priests in a pen beside an altar on the edge of the lake, was now grunting fiercely. His eyes were bloodshot and bulging, and the animal rolled and thrashed on the ground in violent spasms.

The bloody color of the water and the reaction of the boar were an unmistakable prophecy that a cruel war was imminent. The people of the village crowded around the boar's pen, not wanting to believe this terrible omen. The council of the elders assembled quickly to discuss the matter.

First, the elders went about performing the ceremony of recalling the merits of their clans and tribe. They praised the friendliness of their people and celebrated the laws on treating strangers and visitors with hospitality. They talked of their traditional profound respect for their parents and of everyone's commitment to care for the old, the weak, the sick, and the needy. All of this was for the benefit of the gods, lest the gods forget the virtues of their worshippers.

"O gods!" the oldest among the elders cried out as he turned his face up to the sky. "Can you see a beggar among us?"

The gods looked down and could see not a single beggar or poor man left without the support of his neighbors, and the gods had no doubt that those obedient and solicitous

TRADITION OF HOSPITALITY—Quite remarkable are the chronicles which catalogue the benevolent character traits ascribed to the Slavs (for instance, to the Rani), the most prominent ones being hospitality, respect for one's parents, and care of the old, the diseased and the needy. Tradition has it, for example, that there were no mendicants in the Slavic settlement on Rögen Island (today the territory of Germany). This testifies to the high morality of the Pagan Slavs. It was not for nothing that their social-mindedness and altruistic commitment came to be cited as model for their Christian neighbors to emulate.

people deserved their utmost attention. Nevertheless, the gods refused to listen to the urgent pleas of the elders for help. Only for a moment did the gods even pause in their conversations to listen to the pleas, and then they quickly resumed their usual bickering and arguing.

The gods did not like to become involved in the wars of the humans. Occasionally, however, for amusement, a bored deity would yield to the urgent entreaties and help a favorite warrior in skirmishes or battles. Then the thankful warriors would eagerly express their gratitude by offering up sacrifices.

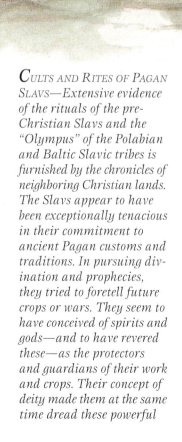

*C*ULTS AND *R*ITES OF *P*AGAN *S*LAVS—*Extensive evidence of the rituals of the pre-Christian Slavs and the "Olympus" of the Polabian and Baltic Slavic tribes is furnished by the chronicles of neighboring Christian lands. The Slavs appear to have been exceptionally tenacious in their commitment to ancient Pagan customs and traditions. In pursuing divination and prophecies, they tried to foretell future crops or wars. They seem to have conceived of spirits and gods—and to have revered these—as the protectors and guardians of their work and crops. Their concept of deity made them at the same time dread these powerful forces, which commanded awe and inspired extreme terror. The Pagan Slavs believed that the divine spirits and forces might destroy all life or punish people with plague, cholera and other dreaded scourges. It is exactly this kind of fear mingled with awe that must have lain at the root of such religious traditions as paying the homage of prayer and sacrifice to gods. Human sacrifices were not uncommonly offered to them to avert their wrath. The most prominent tribal or communal festivals used to be held at the onset of the summer and the harvest. During wars, apart from carrying and wearing sacred insignia, ancient*

Merry Yarovit, having grown bored with the conversations in the Giant Oak, climbed down to one of the lower branches to amuse himself a little with the warriors. He drew aside the thick veil of leaves and was horror-stricken at the sight beneath him. Not believing his eyes, Yarovit looked closer and then still closer before dashing away to tell Svarozhich what he had seen.

The alarm had been sounded and all the gods were there to hear Yarovit's report. A deathly silence filled the tree as Yarovit described the huge hordes of the Nemtsi,

Slavs would bring from Rethra to battle a white horse, believed to be Svarozhich's steed. With no rider on its back, though saddled, the horse was supposed to create the impression among the Slavs that the invisible god himself was fighting by their side. Svantovit's white stallion appears to have been used for like purposes at Arcona, as was Triglav's war horse at Stettin. Tribal deities were largely invoked in connection with tribal or family events like birth, marriage, or death. Divination was widespread down to the latter part of the Twelfth Century.

Valuable gifts are reported to have been sent from all neighboring lands to Svantovit's oracle in the Slavonic Wagria, now the area of Löbeck in Germany, even by non-Slavic neighbors. Proof is provided by a precious goblet donated by Danish King Sven. No one entered a sanctuary but a priest dedicated to the service of the deity. Yet even he could only enter the precinct with his breath bated, and whenever he wanted to take another breath he had to run to the entrance door to inhale. Ritual solemnities used to be followed by grand feasts.

Prince Helmold related his impressions in the Slavic Chronicle like this: "... now I have had an opportunity for experiencing first-hand things I'd earlier just heard of as related by others. What is involved is that there is no other people like the Slavs for extending their hospitality to strangers." The Slavic people were extremely generous to their guests, and their hospitality used to be rather offered than requested. If a member of the Slavic community was exposed as reluctant to welcome a stranger at his home, such a host could expect to have his abode set those that lived outside the Slavic world, overrunning Slavic settlements and killing vast numbers of Slavs. When he had finished, the gods quietly followed Svarozhich up to the very top branches of the Giant Oak to get a good view of the scene unfolding beneath them and fearing a grim outcome for the Slavs.

The supreme god Svarozhich had always been reluctant to interfere with the dispensations of the three Fates, and this time was no exception. Prove grimly had to agree with him. The lamentations of the council of elders, however, did deeply move several of the other gods. Perun was the first to speak, disapproving angrily of Svarozhich's command not to interfere. Svantovit waited silently, shaking his head. Triglav suggested they give aid to both sides so as not to show favoritism and, more importantly, to make the sounds of war as deafening as possible and make the battle one that would live forever in human memory. Young Rugievit, Porenut, and Porevit had been overjoyed to see the battle and longed for a chance to descend to the earth and display their skills and valor in war. Yarilo was outraged, and demanded the right to give the Slavs the aid of his powerful golden shield. This shield could rob the enemy not only of his sight but also of his sense of touch, and could make minds reel so badly that the enemy couldn't even stand up. Yarilo swore and foamed with anger, exhorting the other gods to action, since his favorite season, that of the harvest, was rapidly approaching and the war would wreak havoc on that time of merriment and plenty. Byelobog advised putting the Nemtsi into a hypnotic sleep and letting them wander senseless to get lost in the swamps and marshes. Chernobog laughed maliciously as Lada, Vesna, and Pizamar wept at the feet of Svarozhich and begged him to allow the Slavs some help.

As the gods argued, the council of elders went to consult the oracle about the outcome of the war. The soothsayer kindled a fire and flung his herbs into it so that he could read the fortunes of his people in the smoke. He bowed to the fire and the smoke, and muttering enchantments, began to weep and shriek as he pleaded with the gods. Youths, women, and children huddled close around, hoping for good news. The men couldn't wait for the response, as they had to hurry off to prepare for war. The Nemtsi were drawing ever closer and time was short.

on fire. Moreover, the culprit guilty of any ill-treatment of strangers would be condemned in public for "having denied bread to a stranger …". Besides worshiping their idols and bringing votive objects to their gods, the Slavs, in order to propitiate divine forces, would offer them human sacrifices. The custom decreed that widowed wives and female slaves of a deceased tribal prince

should die and follow him to another world. "Vicarious" sacrificial offerings were also practiced, i.e., when a living animal's likeness—clay statuettes of a horse, a goat or a ram—was brought to a god in its stead. It was the responsibility of temple priests to protect, promote and enforce such cult rites. Faith in the existence of the gods and the powers they wielded affected any major decision on either war or peace as well as in intra- and inter-tribal relations.

Next, the soothsayer sacrificed a rooster to the Father of the Gods, Svarog, since his dreams gave direction to the Fates, and the fortune telling would only be accurate if the Fates had been placated. Afterwards a bull was driven to the sacrificial altar. The temple priest, clothed in his robes and his face painted in loud colors, washed his face in the heavily scented and sticky blood. The smell sent him into a trance, and he began moving and chanting ecstatically, invoking Svantovit, the god of war and fortune telling.

All arms were raised to the sky, and Svantovit's celebrated pure white horse was brought forward. The animal was foaming from a long ride, and the people sighed, taking it as a good sign that Svantovit had been riding that night. Breathlessly they crossed the spears before the horse. But the horse made no attempt to step over them. Impatience and uncertainty ran through the crowd. Then the horse moved, but ominously lifted its left leg, which would mean a lost battle. But it lowered its hoof without stepping forward.

The crowd breathed a small sigh of relief. The priest poked the horse, and this time it went forward over the spears, right foot first. Everyone gave a shout of joy.

The people then left the altar and went to the sacred oak grove to make an offering to the god of good luck. The young children placed the flesh of the sacrificed bull, some wheat, milk, honey, and mead on the exposed roots of the large oak at the center of the grove. The head priest then came forward and invoked the gods Perun, Svarozhich, Svantovit, Prove, Triglav, and Yarovit before placing rough clay statuettes of the Nemtsi on the ground. Softly he sang a cruel song of war as he circled the clay images and then began piercing them with a spear. This act was meant to be a plea to Chernobog to be careful and make no mistakes as he guided the cold hand of Death.

The warriors had gathered by this time, and they all stopped by the sacred groves before heading to the battlefield. They shot arrows and threw their spears at the old oaks, scratching and tearing the hard wood. At each hit, the spectators joyously shouted their appreciation. Other warriors ran to nearby springs to dip their weapons and amulets into the cold, clear water, appealing to the kindly demons of the waters for protection and guidance.

In the meantime the gods were still arguing. They all wanted to help the Slavs but, by their own laws, were forbidden from reversing the decrees of the Fates. Perun was the most vocal, and even Svarozhich listened carefully to his words. But nothing could sway him to change his command.

Within hours the fierce fight had reached the place right under the crown of the Giant Oak itself. More and more souls hovered over the battlefield and barren Death, content, took them in flocks to the kingdom of Veles.

Poor Pripelaga could barely stand all the stamping of horses and stirring dust and moans and groans of the dying and all the other noise and commotion of the battle. Urgently she pleaded with the gods of war to stop helping the warriors recover their strength and encouraging them back into the fight. She turned to Podaga to bring darkness and thick fog to cover the battlefield like a blanket. Pripelaga then begged Svarozhich through teary eyes to whip his golden-maned stallion and hurry the Sun out of the sky to give the warriors the respite of night.

Jubilantly the war gods turned a deaf ear to her appeals and encouraged the bloodshed and butchery. And divine Podaga, sympathetic as she was, would not disobey Svarozhich's command of impartiality. Svarozhich, as much as it pained him, held the reins tight and kept his pace steady. Below him, the victorious cries of the Nemtsi were growing ever louder and more frequent. Ravens, wolves, foxes, and dogs ripped and tore at the dead bodies. The Slavs were forced to keep retreating. It became clear that the prophecy of the white horse had only served to encourage them before a battle they were doomed to lose.

Finally, dusk fell upon the battlefield. Their spirits broken, the Slavic warriors gathered wearily around their flickering campfires to tend to their wounds and try to sleep a little before the morning Aurora once again drove them onto the battlefield. The lament of mothers and new widows could be heard from far off. The moans of the wounded and maimed, as well as the aroma of herbal teas, which helped dull the pain and bring sleep, mixed with the terror of the coming morning.

The gods were quiet in the Giant Oak, slowly sipping their mead as Pizamar reluctantly played a melancholy tune on her flute.

Inevitably the Evening Star, Zorya, began to withdraw to her shelter, and the Morning Star, Rannitsa, came out to take over from her. The rosy-cheeked goddess undid her soft silken red scarf to comb her red hair when she looked down at the battlefield. That morning Aurora shed tears, making all the flowers, trees, meadows, and fields sparkle with dew. Svarozhich, just starting his climb into the sky, became stiff and grimaced when he saw how badly the Slavs had done in the blood bath of the previous day. His divine heart bled for them. Still, he wanted to remain impartial, and so only urged on his horse into the sky.

As the warriors began to get ready for another day of battle, four noble warriors in shining armor suddenly made an appearance among the Slavs. These four went from rank to rank, awakening, exhorting, and giving new hope to the dispirited defenders. Despair sped from the minds of the Slavs, and their bloodshot and tired eyes showed renewed strength and courage.

Suspicious, Svarozhich stood up on the seat of his chariot to get a better look at these mysterious new warriors. The reflection of their armor gave him a clue to their identity, since it was the armor of gods. The three brothers Rugievit, Porenut, and Porevit, along with their cousin Yarovit, had disobeyed the command of Svarozhich and had gone into the camp of the Slavs. They challenged the weary Slavs, urging them on to glory, pouring new hope into their souls, and counseling the Slavs on what they would have to do to be victorious.

Prove was the first god in the Giant Oak to recognize the four new warriors and hurried to let Svarozhich know the truth. Svarozhich knew Prove's complaint was fair, but at that moment he could not leave the celestial chariot unattended. He told Prove to send Sim and Rygl to round up the four and remind them of the punishment they would face for such outrageous disobedience.

Immediately the bird Simargl flew down over the battlefield. There was no way of saying just how much help the brothers and their cousin had been, or if they had even intended staying and helping in the battle, but suddenly a cheerful roar was heard from the camp of the Nemtsi. They had mistaken the hovering Simargl for their goddess

YAROVIT (Gerovit)—A god whose worship on the coast southeast of Rugen Island (now Germany) lingered down to the twelfth century. Written evidence of this is provided by Ebbo and Herbord, official chroniclers of Bishop Otto of Bamberg. Being a war god first and foremost, his warfare aspect was denoted by a large gold shield that hung on the wall of the Slavic shrine described by the bishop's chroniclers. In battle, the god's effigy was carried in front of the infantry to ensure their victory. The chronicle also provides an account of the ceremonies observed at a great vernal festival in honor of this deity in 1128. In addition to his primary

and interpreted her appearance as a sign of their impending victory.

Perun was enraged and his blood boiled. It was true that the Slavs had recovered greatly from the previous day due to the help of the brothers and their cousin, but the joyful shouts from the hordes of Nemtsi was having a dis-heartening effect, and again the Slavs were losing. Furious, Perun bared his teeth.

"It may have been unwitting, but Simargl has actually helped the Nemtsi!" he roared. "That is neither fair nor right!"

He hesitated no more. Drawing back his powerful arm, Perun hurled a mighty bolt of lightning down on the leader of the Nemtsi. Then he threw another and another, again and again. The wagons of the Nemtsi caught fire and blazed like torches. Their horses fell to their knees

war functions, this god per-sonified the annual revival of plant life. The aim of this festival would have been to placate the powers that controlled the rebirth of food sources in the spring. This god's existence is also supported by the Danish chronicler Saxo Grammaticus

under the loud claps of thunder. In vain, Svarozhich leapt from his chariot, but he was too late and could only throw up his hands at Perun's unprecedented boldness. The struggle had taken a new turn. Perun turned to Podaga and forbade her let even a single drop of rain fall to the earth. Only his blows continued to fall from the sky like the strokes of a fiery battle-axe. The Slavs raised their heads and stared up at the heavens in wonder.

What Insulted the
VICTORIOUS SLAVS
in their Finest Hour

The savage battle lasted one more day. At nightfall, the clamor of war finally died away, and the Slavic warriors pursued the Nemtsi as they dispersed in all directions. Those that were captured became slaves. The warriors enjoyed the chase after the fierce fighting, but were amazed when one of their prisoners could answer them in their own language. They had never been able to understand the strange noises of the Nemtsi and had thought them dumb, but here they had one that could talk with the Slavs easily.

At the victory celebration, the Slavs gratefully made sacrifice after sacrifice to their gods. When they had honored all the gods, they held a lavish banquet where the spoils of war were divided, followed by entertainment and games.

But the indisputable focus of attention was the strange captive who could speak the Slavic language. He told his story, how he had been found in the woods by the Nemtsi as a young boy, and how the Nemtsi had adopted him and brought him up as one of their own.

"Do you mean the *Nemtsi*? The dumb?" inquired one of the elders. The elders had grown accustomed to calling all outsiders dumb, since they could not converse with them.

"That's not what they call themselves," the prisoner answered. "And they are not dumb, either. You simply do not understand their language, just as they do not understand yours. They consider you to be dumb."

The onlookers grumbled disapprovingly, and jeers came from the large crowd.

"They have their own tongue, and they do not want to conquer your land. They just want to reach theirs to settle."

The discontented crowd booed again. After all, they had no reason to believe the prisoner had really been found in the woods as a boy. He could just as easily have joined the Nemtsi of his own free will. And the suggestion that the ancestors of the Slavs had taken their land away from the Nemtsi angered the people even more. The crowd grew more vocal and had to be calmed by the raised right hand of one of the elders.

"We haven't occupied anyone's territory, we live where our grandfathers and great-grandfathers lived before us," a gray-haired old man told the youth sternly. Some people shouted threats at the captive.

"Our people, and by that I mean the people that raised me, say that you come from very far away, from whence the sun rises," the youth replied. He looked out over the crowd, perplexed that they had laughed at these words.

The old man raised his hand again to silence the crowd.

"And the Sun you worship is a false god," added the obstinate prisoner. A threatening and ominous silence fell over the crowd. In a soft voice, the youth continued, "It is Thor, the giant son of Odin and Frigga, who is a true god."

The onlookers would have assaulted him and torn him to pieces right then if it had not been for the calm presence of the wise elders.

"See, he is young. And not very smart, either," said the oldest of the elders, before he rose to send the crowd away.

When the elders and the priests were left alone with the prisoner, the old man addressed the captive again, in a gentle manner. "Now, we would like to hear more about the quarter of the world you come from. That we can understand one another is quite a remarkable thing. What is the word for 'hand' in your language?"

The prisoner answered him quickly.

"And for 'head'? 'Leg'? A tree?" The elders bombarded the youth with questions, and he had no trouble answering any of them.

"Couldn't he be lying?" asked one of the priests.

The priests urged the elders to ask the prisoner about more important things that they were eager to learn. They wanted to know how far away the home of the foreigners was, how rich the people were, and how many of them there were. And the priests bristled with anger every time the prisoner mentioned his strange, unknown gods. A long time before the Slavs had been visited by some people from far southern lands that claimed that there was only one true god for everyone to worship, and they had laughed at those people and sent them

back to their own lands. But this captive was full of pride for his gods, and that drew the ire of the priests. Indignant, they branded him a shameless liar and demanded his death.

"Why not sacrifice him to the gods for their assistance to our victory in this war?" ventured the youngest and most impatient of the priests.

The wise elders knitted their brows.

"His self-conceit and arrogance will prove fatal to him," proclaimed another of the priests.

"He has insulted our gods. You will never get people to forget this or prevent the children from spitting and throwing stones at him," declared yet another priest. "Worse yet, do not forget how many of our own have perished by his murderous hand!"

The council of elders took a long time to consult on the fate of the prisoner, as they were in no hurry to order the man to his death. It had been many years since they had offered a human sacrifice to the gods. But there was no doubt that the prisoner deserved such an end, as he had spilled the blood of their relatives and loved ones, and then insulted their gods.

So the elders ruled, "The prisoner will be exposed to trial by the gods. We have overcome in this war, our gods have helped us to victory, so there can be no challenging their greatness. But we have lost some wars in the past, and we may not emerge victorious in all of the battles we will fight in the future. It would be too daring and insulting to beseech our gods to prove their greatness once more, therefore this tribunal will not try to decide whether our gods are in the right or whether this shameless young man is telling the truth. We will only place his life at the mercy of the gods. It is up to them to decide whether he deserves death for his sacrilege or whether he should be forgiven for his impudence. Should the latter be the case, the prisoner will be the property of this temple."

The priests did not like the verdict, since the stranger could easily end up a gift to the temple, and that was something that could not be rejected. He had been offered as part of the spoils of war, and it would violate custom to reject him, no matter how much the priests despised him. But first the prisoner had to be submitted to a divine trial, and for that the priests chose ordeal by fire.

"If he is telling the truth, our gods, who are fair and just, will spare his life," whispered the more reasonable warriors, who were not ashamed to admire the courage of the youth. They had long known that people in foreign countries worshipped false gods who were sometimes very similar to their own deities, though the warriors thought those false gods seemed much more cruel.

"You will see that he will not pass the trial," the priests said, trying to persuade any who would listen. The blasphemous ideas of the prisoner had them truly scared. "This unworthy liar has insulted our gods on our land, therefore he will be sacrificed. But in doing so we are showing this bold foreigner great respect, since his soul will become one of the Planetarians, the planet spirits that assist our gods."

The ordeal by fire took place immediately. The priests prepared the fiery paths and implored the gods to confirm their power in this trial. The whole village had gathered to watch, and many in the crowd now looked at the brave young prisoner with respect and compassion.

But the prisoner did not emerge victorious from this tortuous trial of the just and fair gods. He failed to finish the entire length of the last fiery path. The young man fainted before he could finish, and the sizzling flames gnawed at his youthful body. The spectators did not shout for joy, but neither did they feel sorry for the foreigner. Most agreed with the priests that the prisoner's future as a Planetarian was not the worst fate that could befall a man.

The head priest slew a lamb and then a calf, and both were bloody and cruel sacrifices. They brought the young prisoner forward and served him a strong potion that woke him up and made his head reel. Carefully they raised him up to the crown of an oak tree and fastened a rope around his neck. The prisoner shuddered. The priests struck up a plaintive song. The dirge rose through the branches of the tree and reached the upper branches of the Giant Oak, where the gods received the victim's soul from their devout worshippers. This is how

a foreigner became one of the Planetarians, who are the souls of people who have been sacrificed to the gods and then appointed guardians of the twinkling star lights.

Afterwards, the priests divided the spoils of war. The major share went to the temple, and then the elders gave gifts to those who had lost their loved ones, and most importantly, to widows with young children. The warriors who had returned shared what remained. There were no complaints, even from those who were left empty-handed. They were glad that their lives had been spared and the gods had allowed them to return to their loved ones. Then the minstrels sang, and the festival began.

In the morning, the priests lowered the stranger's body from the tree, where it had remained through the night, and erected a huge pile of stones in the forest to honor and mark his burial place. This act marked the end of the feast and the celebration of the great victory.

Why the
GODS HIDE THEMSELVES

After a time the people began to grow conceited as they unveiled one secret of the gods after another. Since all the secrets bear on one another, the Slavs were even able, through clever application, to discover some secrets that the gods hadn't revealed to them. Many such accomplishments led the people to believe that they had become the equals of the gods, and piece by piece, they started giving up the faith of their forefathers. Presumptuous, they finally stopped invoking the gods altogether. This treacherous neglect proved fateful.

When hordes of the Nemtsi returned the gods no longer offered support, and the foreign invaders conquered the Slavic lands, usurping control and imposing on the people a new faith. The invaders burnt down homes and palisades. Even worse, they reduced to ashes many of the sacred oak groves and desecrated the shrines. They tore down the idols of the ancient gods and destroyed the gods' temples or put up new divinities in those shrines.

The once revered gods were horrified at the arrogance and lack of deference on the part of the Slavs. And the gods showed little compassion for the people, recognizing that the Slavs had driven themselves into servitude and willingly exchanged their freedom and independence for the life of prisoners and slaves, of submissive servants and maids.

Filled with a sense of outrage, the gods gave up all attempts to curb the cruelty of the Fates and let their full fury attack the people. As a result, the people came to be haunted by all manner of misfortune and peril. Strange and unheard-of diseases plagued them, new and brutal wars that killed not only warriors but also the women

and children and spread famine and hunger, became
common. Humiliation and misery were widespread, and
deprivation and hardship became the usual circumstances
of the lives of the Slavs.

The gods were sickened by the weakness and wicked-
ness of the people, as well as by their inability to protect
themselves and the images of the gods, and resolved to
have even less to do with the people. To withdraw from
the people even further, the gods taught many things to
the demons and lesser divinities, and gave over responsibility for many earthly matters to the demons.

That left the demons free to settle for good in the
minds of the people, in their everyday business, in their
toil, their leisure, and even their births and deaths. Not all
of the demons, however, chose to follow the instructions
of the gods and many chose to harm rather than help the
people. Many battles were fought between the benevolent
demons and the wicked ones over this.

Many of the demons, despite never having been seen
by human eyes, came to be well known for the kind
things they would do for people. Kovlad the Iron-Keeper
and his wife Runa, the mistress of the earth, and their servants the Permoniks, or kobolds, were known to be
benevolent demons. Others included the King and Queen
of the Sea and their sea fairies and water vile; the King
and Queen of Waters and Rivers; the cloud-giver
Oblachnik, the Lord of the Winds; his brother Frost; the
whistling Pohvizd, father of the winds; his wife
Veternitsa; two of their sons, Vanok, or Breeze, and the
gentle Vetrik, or Fan; the Sun and the Moon; rosy-
cheeked Aurora, who appears in the morning as Rannitsa
the Morning Star and in the evening as Vetchernitsa the
Evening Star; the colorful Rainbow, who is the child of
the Sun and the goddess Podaga; the King of Time, who is
the father of the Twelve Months or Little Moons and
must keep revolving on his mill stone; Good Luck, the
kindest of the three Fates; Lesovik, the Lord of the Woods;
Rye Old Father, the guardian spirit of the fields; Domovik,
or Gazdichko, who looks after the welfare of the household aided by Chlevnik the cattle-shed hand, Humnik the

threshing-floor hand, the wine-tasting Vintsurik, Pikulik the Sweet Tooth, who helps wagon men, and Korgorusha, who appears in the guise of a cat.

The other demons were evil and deliberately harmed people out of spite. Laktibrada, a tiny, malicious dwarf, delighted in people's ordeals. Yudas, the black water vile, would drown enthusiastic and reckless swimmers. The

green-haired spirits of the lakes and ponds, along with the lonely water vile Samodivas, also liked to pull people under water if they ventured too close. The younger sons and daughters of Pohvizd, the father of the Winds, caused nothing but trouble. They include Vikhor', or Whirlwind, Smrsht', or Storm Wind, Hurricane, Meluzina the Howling Wind, and Metelitsa the Blizzard. The witch Baba Yaga and her brother, the wizard Strigon', generally liked to cause mischief, but could take a liking to someone occasionally and offer help. But people always knew to stay away from the demons of fire such as the Fiery Man, Svetlonos with his lantern, and the evil sprites Zmock and Rarashik, who had bad manners and evil designs. The nocturnal fairy Polnochnitsa the Midnight Guest struck fear in the hearts of the people she visited, since one member of the household would always die shortly afterward, as she was sent by Death herself to spy. Krachun, the Master of the Winter Solstice, would murder people out of a passion to kill simply for forgetting to set a badniak, his favorite tree trunk, on fire. Poludnitsa the Midday Guest delighted in punishing people and preventing them from working in their fields during the middle of the day. Mamuna, helped by the fairies, would torture and tantalize the naive to death. The little snake Hadovik and Weasel would often fight with the benevolent household demons because they loved to cause harm to family and property. Nasty Kikimora enjoyed hurting men, injuring animals, and even tangling women's yarn. The rogue Madra would talk those of weak character into crime, who were then helped by the specters Matoha and Mora the Nightmare, as well as by Upir the Vampire and Vlkodlak the Werewolf. And Labus the Enticer, who delighted in luring children into caves, came to be feared by the people that lived near the mountains.

By and by the people let the old ways and customs fall into oblivion. At the same time they were increasingly coerced into renouncing their ancient faith and worshipping the new highest gods. New minor divinities were also proposed and imposed, taking the form of demons, saints, and prophets. The gods of the early Slavs were pleased with what was taking place, since the people were being punished by their own folly. They let themselves be governed and lured away by so many new and strange agencies that they could no longer recognize what they could or should believe. And the ancient gods sat undisturbed in the Giant Oak, feasting and celebrating, no longer caring about the fate of the people.

The gods now while away their divine time in different ways. Perun keeps hurling down his bolts of lightning and crashing his deafening peals of thunder. Svarozhich still takes his daily ride across the sky with the precious Sun-egg. Only Chmarnik, who delights in gathering heavy clouds, keeps poisoning his solar life. War-mongering Triglav and the other gods of war are not bored either, as they continue to sow seeds of dissension, playing havoc with the world and bringing misery and sorrow to the human race. Death never lags far behind, as there is still much work for her to do. And Prove's daughters, the Fates of Good Luck,

Misery, and Revenge, are often so busy they are not sure what to attend to.

Patiently the gods amuse themselves as they wait in the Giant Oak, knowing that someday they will recover the esteem of the people and receive their due homage again. People, as a matter of fact, have shown their most

recent gods and demons less and less appreciation and, ever ungrateful, they will sooner or later turn away from them as well.

But the ancestral gods are not malicious. They are simply waiting, hidden in the crown of the wondrous Giant Oak, untouched by human inattention and neglect. And they are not waiting in vain, since they are only too aware of the mysteries that they have not yet revealed and that humans have not discovered, but which the human race will someday have a need to learn.

Afterword
THE SLAVS AND SLAVDOM

Figure #1

Where did they come from? What is their racial identity? How did they shape their own history and their social institutions? Answers to these and a whole host of other related questions have been sought by interdisciplinary Slavonic studies. Although the beginnings of the Slavs (who at some point in their development started calling themselves Slovenes/Sloviens, which the Romans transcribed as Sclavini, Sclavi, Slavi) seemed to have been irretrievably lost in the remote past of their prehistoric development, piece by piece the mosaic of scattered knowledge has been gathered up and fitted together. Isolated references across historic records have shed new light on their early history. The missing information has been supplemented by linguistic research and particularly by the 'silent and anonymous' artifacts unearthed during archeological explorations.

Two scholarly theories, and various modifications thereof, have in the last two centuries sought to substantiate the arrival of the Slavic tribes at a point in time which is illuminated by written evidence and distinguished by the massive migratory waves of contemporary tribes. These massive population shifts occurred in the Fifth Century AD. An indigenous theory argues that the Slavic tribes had permanently inhabited the same territory subsequently attested as theirs in historic annals along with their tribal names. A migratory theory of the Slavs' origins claims that the initial homeland of the Early Slavs must have been somewhere either north or north-east of the Carpathian Mountains, whence they spread to colonize the lands historically accorded the Slavonic nations. Another theory appears to adopt a conventional approach in building its case, i.e., some kind of original homeland—migratory movements—historic advent of the Slavs. It seems sensible to suggest that one may not entirely agree with or reject outright the inferences of either theory. It may well be that the truth resides somewhere in between.

The traditional claim that the Slavs migrated at some point in their pre-history into their historically acknowledged settlements has been challenged, if not entirely refuted, by the most recent scholarship. To start with, it appears most unlikely that there could have existed, at the turn of the Fifth Century AD, within a much coveted European heartland (so central to the concerns and appetites of early historic and early medieval ethnic groupings) a no-man's land left vacant and unattended for some migratory agricultural tribes of Slavs to come, see and settle it. This lingering concept is rooted in the previous century, which was marked by the domination of ideas advanced by German historiography and the German linguistic school. The period map of ancient and early medieval Europe had been largely designed in compliance with the said prevalent notions and concepts. This 'period' map did not fail to identify and position with an amazing degree of certainty the so called historic nations while relegating the Slavs to fringe territories. As their living space, the Early Slavs had been 'allotted' lands on marginal and peripheral areas.

Given the very few references on the Slavs in the texts of Antiquity, the original home of the Sclavini/Slovenes and their nation-creating process ('ethnogenesis') has been the subject of endless discussion. The topic we are concerned with touches on two disputed areas: the geographic location of the Slavs' prehistoric cradle and the chronology of their subsequent expansion. More specifically, we are curious as to when the Slavic southward and westward migration into Europe began. One widely accepted claim is that 'the Slavs entered European history as late as the middle of the first millennium AD…'.

Many conventional opinions on Slavic expansion into central, eastern and southern Europe stem from the enduring misconception of European cultural and spiritual dualism symbolized by the advanced Roman-German (Teutonic) area and the backward Graeco-Slavic one. These concepts once developed and propagated by the proponents of Nineteenth Century Romanticism were, regrettably, adopted by sizeable sections of the Slavonic cultural community and intellectuals. The ideas of alleged Slavic and Slavonic inferiority have adversely affected Slavic self-consciousness and self-esteem. In

Figure #2

view of the above, it comes as no surprise that, following the great migration of peoples throughout Europe, the Slavic tribes were accorded a fairly unimaginative material culture, which was allegedly the accurate reflection of their living standards, as well as a proof of their negligible "contribution" to European civilization. It is commonly forgotten that the period was one of overall economic and cultural decline brought about by political changes following the fall of the Roman Empire and the decline of its once thriving provinces. Their plight was exacerbated by frequent military inroads and movements by multiple ethnic groups heading for the south and west of the European continent. The profound maladies the Roman Empire was suffering, as well as its subsequent waning and collapse, entailed the crisis of the so-called barbaric regions lying north of the Roman boundary or *Limes Romanus.* Not only was this social and political turmoil responsible for the transitory decline in the region but also for the long-range economic stagnation and cultural decay affecting the whole European heartland, including the Carpathian Basin and the drainage area of the River Danube or the Danubian Plain.

The original homeland of the Slavs spread not only across extensive reaches stretching along such rivers as the Oder, the Vistula, the Dnieper, the Dniester and the Bug, but also (on the most recent linguistic research) throughout the Carpathian Basin. I share this hypothesis with the historian and ethnographer Pavol Jozef Šafárik, who calls the area under discussion 'the Middle Danubian Area'. It was in this geographical setting that the Slavic tribes were destined to shape themselves and be shaped by others around the middle of the first millennium of our era. At this point (with the movement of the Huns, the Gepids, the Langobards and other ethnic groupings lured by the easily-accessible riches of ancient Rome), the Slavic tribes found themselves involved in this huge migratory surge driving them farther away from the Transcarpathian and Carpathian regions towards the more southerly and more westerly corners of crumbling ancient Europe.

The Slavs maintained lively contacts with the Balts in the north, the steppe ethnic groups in the east and south-east, the ancient and post-ancient world in the south, as well as the emerging civilization of the Germanic/Teutonic tribes in the west. The geographical position enjoyed by the Slavs was a major factor in shaping their cultural fabric and promoting their economic-political organization. Owing to the multifarious contacts established at all the cardinal points of the compass, the initial relative 'homogeneity' of the ancient Slavic tribes gradually metamorphosed into the heterogeneous plurality of distinct cultural enclaves, tribal groups and first germs of early medieval Slavic super-tribal and, in the final effect, state formations. These geographical surroundings proved to be a remarkably auspicious one for the emergence of the most ancient state unit of the Western Slavs and the Moravian Slavs (Sloviens/Sclavi Margenses). A very similar statehood pattern was reiterated in more southerly European areas, where, in affinity with the ancient civilization and the Byzantine Empire, the common state of the Slavs and Early Bulgars made its appearance. The politics and policies of independence and autonomy at this time typify the political endeavor of the Pannonic and Dalmatian Croats, the Carinthian Slavs and the Sorbs. Another testimony to the said trend is the creation of the Sorbian princedom, Rashka, and that of the Croats in Dalmatia.

By the end of the migration of nations, the Carpathian Sloviens/Sclavini had emerged as the stock of the Western Slav, as well as in part of the Southern Slavic tribes in the original Slavic homeland. These ethnic groupings settled the area of the Middle Danube River and created in this area a suitable economic and social basis for their first-ever state structure, Samo's Empire, Samo being a Frankish merchant and warlord. More remarkably, the ancient Slavic state was established as early as the Seventh Century AD. Samo, a rallying figure and 'the first in a series of individuals in Slovak history whose contribution is quite singular', ruled successfully for thirty-five years. His landmark accomplishment of organizing the

Slavs into a kingdom may have been due, apart from his own exceptional talents and daring, to a happy concourse of circumstance. The Early Slavs successfully maintained some of Europe's oldest and most historic roads and the water trade route provided by the Danube River, Europe's major waterway. Samo's Empire, a defensive union, was a strong organization with considerable vitality and military strength for defending itself from assaults by the nomadic Avars and from the claims of the Frankish feudal lords who kept harassing the lands of the Slavs. These saw their eastward expansion seriously threatened by the very existence of the ever mightier Slavic kingdom. This first politically organized community of the Sclaveni/Slavs continued to be held in esteem long after its dismemberment and the subsequent appearance of the Avar Khaganate, with some parts of Samo's Empire as its constituents. New political agreements probably allowed the ancient Slavs to exercise some form of autonomy and edify their country to become the scene of noteworthy historical political processes and the epoch-making mission of the great scholars and saints, Cyril and Methodius.

The Slovieni alias Slovenes alias Sclaveni (a name which around this time is still used to denote Slavic tribes with no own ethnic name; later it will be associated with the Slavs inhabiting the Principality of Nitra) and the Avars entered into a semblance of a cultural and economic alliance, verging on a sort of mutuality. With the Franks bringing pressure to bear on the two tribal societies in the course of the Eighth Century, the allies kept together, gradually merging. Later on in history the Avars were to become Slovienicized through being absorbed by a more vital Slovienian ethnic community, which was laying the foundations of its Principalities of Nitra and Moravia. These super-tribal entities had obviously been arranged in compliance with Christian values as these were pursued in the Ninth Century. Small surprise, then, that the most ancient and historically the most important Slavic state was formed just in this setting. Admittedly, its emergence was prompted and ensured by perspicacious "politicians" such as princes Pribina, Mojmir, Rastislav and Svatopluk I, and enthusiastic promoters of spiritual Christian values like Adalram, Sts Cyril and Methodius, as well as their disciples and opponents (grouped around the towering figure of Bishop Viching). But one may not underestimate the part played by the auspicious economic situation, trade and cultural contacts with the Western and Eastern worlds. Great Moravia, at that time of competing power interests represented by Rome and Byzantium, served as a bridge between the two, allowing their interaction. The singularity of this period has been neatly captured by the prominent Slovak writer of the Twentieth Century Vladimir Minac. He wrote nearly thirty years ago that 'creation of the vernacular and its protection

was an absolutely fundamental historic fact…, virtually the most central political motive of Great Moravia and obviously an accomplishment with far-reaching implications for Europe's political and cultural history'.

The legacy of Great Moravian cultural values lingered right to the late Middle Ages, contributing its fine fibers to the spiritual-cultural fabric of the feudal Europe, particularly the Slavonic world. Nobody doubts nowadays that old Slavonic (Slovenian/Slovene) Christian script and oral tradition, as well as the original intellectual streams, dexterity in crafts and natural artistic aptitude of our Slavic ancestors facilitated the creation of the Bulgarian, Polish and the Czech states, as well as Croatia and Kievan Rus'. Last, but not least, the ancient Slavs substantially contributed to the emergence and consolidation of the feudal Hungarian Kingdom (in whose history the destiny of the modern Slovak nation was intertwined until the Twentieth Century). Through-out long centuries to come occupants of this part of European space would cherish the edifying

Figure #3

memories of the Great Moravian Empire which had superseded looser tribal organizations. These memories were ultimately to give spiritual substance to the birth and consolidation of the medieval Slovak ethnic. This national community was, in turn, destined to survive against all odds and uncoil into a modern Slovak people who were, in the long run—in the Twentieth Century—to exercise full sovereignty and a statehood of their own.

Cult worship of gods was an inextricable part of everyday life typifying the ancient Slavs. Research into this area is, however, largely barred, due to either the silence on this subject by classical authors or the paucity and fragmentary character of the historical evidence at our disposal. The ancient Slavic mind was open to nature and the material manifestations of weather, blooming and withering undergone by nature, as well as its chthonic procreativeness, aggression and overkill.

Figure #4

The Slavic world of thought, imagination and imagery (every god is an idol, literally an 'image'; Latin *idolum* from Greek *eidolon*), intimately linked with the prehistoric and historic destiny of the landscape, and the spiritual outlook of its occupants were infinitely rich. This claim has been supported by plentiful archeological finds—artifacts employed in observing heathen Slavic cults and rituals, now either long forgotten or superseded by their later variants. Paganism, along with its cultic exhibitionism, was progressively eroded, above all in the areas adjoining Christendom, due to direct and intensive commerce, which facilitated the infiltration of the new religious doctrine and the ensuing accommodation of the monotheistic principle. But even in these lands immediately exposed to the new religious content (particularly in southern and central Europe), the population continued to observe old heathen customs and rituals secretly, passing these practices down from generation to generation. Christianity superseded and superimposed itself on these heathen beliefs piecemeal, thinning their lurid sensationalism with new interpretations and beliefs. The early pagan Slavs are known, e.g., to have extensively celebrated Christmas, which they held to be the most prominent festival of the year, for at this time "the old Sun leaves and the new is born". Christianity, in the effort to wipe out paganism's earthly glamors and make spirituality primary, filled this holiday with richer connotations reflected in the biblical message of 'God's-grace-to-all-people-of-good-will'. In this way Christianity borrowed many (visually intensive) Pagan rituals, Slavic ones included, then modifying these (cf. saints' corpses under glass, tattered limb bones in gold reliquaries, half-nude St Sebastian pierced by arrows, St Lucy holding her eyeballs out on a platter, etc.) by infusing them with new ideas, accents and the basically more human, humane and humanitarian message of the New Testament.

More to the north and the east of Europe, Slavic pagan cults, customs and rituals lingered down to the Eleventh and Twelfth Centuries. Heathen religion became amongst the Slavs of the Baltic region a sort of established state ideology. The extent to which a deity was worshipped was coextensive with the powers exercised by this or that ruler. In Pomerania (present day Poland) and among the Baltic Slavs, e.g., the influence of native divinities was contingent on the economic position of a given municipality or a sanctuary. Polytheistic in character, the religion of the Polabian Slavs was too drained of its primeval sap to successfully withstand military or ideological clashes and encounters with the more progressive Christian world. Unfortunately, during the Middle Ages the Slavic Baltic and Polabian tribes were, unlike other still thriving ethnic groupings, Germanized and, due to ethnic isolation, did share the fate of the ancient Celts. With the exception of tiny islets of the Lusatian Sorbs who made up small droplets of Slavdom in the sea of the Germanic cultural setting, the remainder of these tribes ceased to exist as distinctive ethnic entities.

The opinions of the scholars of the cults and rituals of the Early Slavs substantially diverge. Some maintain that the early Slavic tribes had no gods in the strict sense of the word, i.e., with their various anthropomorphic functions clearly defined. It had been long presumed that the pagan Slavs had recognized, honored and feared in their original prehistoric homeland divine spirits of various sorts, the majority thereof being of lower status or demons (pan-demonism thesis). These creatures served as the embodiment and vivification of natural phenomena (animism); some of these divine spirits were believed to be the souls of dead ancestors (maneism). Holders of said views would argue that notions of gods could not have taken shape until the influence of Christianity, specifically through a sort of promotion of certain plants and vegetative elements (as well as prominent ancestors) to a higher anthropomorphic status or sphere where natural phenomena and objects were invested with human qualities, some of the former being raised to deity.

The Czech scholar Zdenek Vana seeks to prove that the Slavs in their early beginnings did pursue polytheism, which suggests that they went through the same nation-creating process ('ethnogenesis') ascribed to other prehistoric European tribes. The prehistoric Slavs did recognize the existence of a set of divinities with their assigned, though all too often overlapping, functions. These things are proved on the authority of the Byzantine historian Procopius of Ceasareia, who wrote in the Sixth Century that the Slavs (judging by the description of the tribes and ethnic groups he referred to, the historian meant the Slavs) showed the utmost reverence to the thunder-god, the chief god surnamed the Thunderbolt; this Slavic deity was known to resemble his Greek counterpart Zeus, the Roman thunder-god Jupiter, and the foremost Norse and German deity Thor, Donar or Thunar.

127

Figure #5

The spiritual world and imagery of the Early Slavs was fabulously rich. They left Europe a unique and precious cultural legacy which enriched the medieval civilization of the Old World. Receptive to stimuli coming from all around ancient Europe, the Slavonic people, both in their pagan and Christian stage, were also immediately involved in establishing, via their singular contribution, early traditions and cultural precedents which helped Europe assume its sophisticated and sumptuously embroidered character. The history of the Slavs is actually a continuum of seesawing events, where advances, leaps and golden hours alternated with times of decline, trials and bitter setbacks. The feats and defeats of the Slavic people are incised on the very body of European history.

DUSAN CAPLOVIC
Slovak Academy of Sciences

Figures 1–6: Courtesy of the Slovak Archaeological Institute, Nitra, Slovakia.

Figure 1: Two-headed wooden idol from the eleventh–twelfth century near Fischerinsel, Tollensee, Germany.

Figure 2: Idol almost three meters high of the god Svantovit carved in stone, found in 1848 in the river Zbrucz near Husiatyn, Poland.

Figure 3: Wooden figure of either the god Triglav or Svantovit from the tenth century, near the River Zbrucz by Husiatyn, Poland.

Figure 4: Wooden idol—fertility cult, from second half of the sixth century, Altfriesack, Germany.

Figure 5: Painted clay eggs—called "pisanky" from the tenth century, Kiev, Ukraine.

Figure 6: Small lead horse figure from the eleventh century, Brandenburg, Germany.

Figure #6

See especially: CURTA, F. for the current scholarship and comprehensive bibliography; PAULINY, J. for Arab sources on Slavic myths; DIXON-KENEDY, M. for encyclopedic information and recent bibliography; and KULIKOWSKI, M. for a comprehensive bibliography of works published before 1989.

Alexinsky, G. "Slavic Mythology." *Larousse Encyclopedia of Mythology*. New York, Prometheus Press, 1959, pp 293–310.

Anichkov, E. "Old Russian Pagan Cults." *Transactions of the 3rd International Congress for the History of Religions*, Oxford, 1908, vol. 2, pp 244–60.

Chadwick, N. "The treaties with Greek and Russian Heathenism." *The Beginning of Russian History.* Cambridge, Cambridge University Press, 1946, pp 76–97.

Chernetsov, A.V. "Medieval Russian Pictorial Materials on Paganism and Superstitions." *Slavica Gandensia,* 7–8 (1980–81) pp 99–112.

Cross, S. "The Russian Primary Chronicle." *Harvard Studies and Notes in Philology and Literature,* vol. 12. Cambridge, Harvard University Press, 1930, pp 75–320.

Cross, S. "The Russian Primary Chronicle: Laurentian Text." *The Medieval Academy of America Publications,* no. 60. Cambridge, Harvard University Press, 1953.

Curta, F. *Making an Early Medieval* Ethnie: *The Case of the Early Slavs (Sixth to Seventh Century A.D.).* Ph.D. dissertation, Western Michigan University, 1998, 2 vols.

Curtin, J. *Myths and Folk-Tales of the Russians, Western Slavs and Magyars.* Boston, Little, Brown & Co., 1890.

Dixon-Kenedey, M. *Encyclopedia of Russian and Slavic Myth and Legend.* Santa Barbara, ABC-CLIO, Inc., 1998.

Dvornik, F. *The Slavs in European History and Civilization.* New Brunswick, Rutgers University Press, 1962.

Dvornik, F. *The Slavs: Their Early History and Civilization.* Boston, American Academy of Arts and Sciences, 1956.

Ebbo and Herbordus, *The Life of Otto, Apostle of Pomerania, 1060–1139, by Ebbo and Herbordus.* Translated by C. H. Robinson. London, New York, 1920.

Gieysztor, A. "The Slavic Pantheon and New Comparative Mythology." *Quaestiones Medii Aevi,* 1 (1977) pp 7–32.

Gieysztor, A. "The Slavic Pantheon and the New Comparative Mythology." Harvard University. Seminar on Ukrainian Studies. Minutes. 5 (1974–75) pp 82–84.

Gimbutas, M. "Ancient Slavic Religion: A Synopsis." *To Honor Roman Jakobson. Essays on the Occasion of His Seventieth Birthday, 11 October 1966.* The Hague, Paris, Mouton 1967, vol. 1, pp 738–59.

Gimbutas, M. "Perkunas/Perun, the Thunder God of the Balts and the Slavs." *Journal of Indo-European Studies,* 1 (1973) pp 466–78.

Gimbutas, M. "Religion." *The Slavs.* New York, Praeger, 1971, pp 151–70.

Harkins, W. *Bibliography of Slavic Folk Literature.* New York, Kings Crown Press, 1953.

Helmoldus, *The Chronicle of the Slavs by Helmold, Priest of Bosau.* Translated with introduction and notes by F. J. Tschan. New York, Columbia University Press, 1935.

Hodál, J. *O pohanskom náboženstve starých Slovákov.* Trnava. Nákl. Spolku Sv. Vojtecha, 1925.

Hopkins, E. "Religion of the Slavic Peoples." *History of Religions.* New York, 1918, pp 138–48.

Jakobson, R. "The Slavic God Veles and His Indo-European Cognates." *Studi linguistici in onore Vittore Pisani.* Torino, Paideia, 1969, pp 579–99.

Jakobson, R. "Slavic Mythology." *Funk & Wagnalls Standard Dictionary of Folklore, Myth and Legend.* vol. 2. New York, Funk & Wagnalls, 1950, pp 1025–1028.

Kulikowski, M. A. *Bibliography of Slavic Mythology.* Columbus, Slavica Publishers, 1989.

Kuzmik, J. *Slovnik starovekych a stredovekych autorov, pramenov a kniznych skriptorov so slovenskymi vztahmi = Lexicon auctorum, fontium et scriptorum librorum cum relationibus slovacis antiqui mediique aevi.* Martin, Matica slovenska, 1983.

Lockwood, Y. *Yugoslav Folklore: An Annotated Bibliography of Contributions in English.* San Francisco, R & E Research Associates, 1976.

Machal, J. "Slavic Mythology." *Mythology of All Races.* Boston, Marshall Jones Co., 1918, vol. 3, pp 253–69.

Meyer, K. "Slavic Religion." *Die Religionen der Erde.* Munich, F. Bruckmann, 1927, pp 261–72.

Nagy, G. "Perkunas and Perun." *Antiquitates Indogermanicae. Studien zur indogerman. Altertumskunde u. zur Sprach und Kulturgeschichte d. indogerman. Voelker.* Innsbruck, Inst. für Sprachwissenschaft d. Univ. Innsbruck, 1974, pp 113–31.

Oinas, F. *Essays on Russian Folklore and Mythology.* Columbus, Slavica Publishers, 1985.

Pauliny, J. *Arabské správy o Slovanoch.* Veda, Bratislava, 1999.

Pettazzoni, R. "The Slavs." *The All Knowing God.* London, Methuen, 1956, pp 234–55.

Pettazzoni, R. "West Slavic Paganism." *Essays on the History of Religion.* Leiden, Brill, 1954, pp 151–63

Procopius of Caesarea, *Procopius,* with an English translation by H. B. Dewing. London & New York, The Loeb Classical Library, 1924.

Ralston, W. *The Songs of the Russian People, as Illustrative of Slavonic Mythology and Russian Social Life.* London. Ellis & Green, 1872.

Rybakov, B. "Paganism in Mediaeval Rus," *Social Science,* 6, 1975, no. 1, pp 130–56.

Sadnik, L. "Ancient Slav Religion in the Light of Recent Research," *Eastern Review,* 1. 1948, no.1 pp 36–43.

Schoeps, H. "Slavic Religion." *Religions of Mankind.* Garden City, Doubleday, 1966, pp 112–6.

Sedov, V. "Pagan Sanctuaries and Idols of the Estern Slavs," *Slavica Gandensia,* 7–8 (1980–81) pp 69–85.

Sokolov, J. M. *Russian Folklore.* Translated by C. H. Smith, New York, MacMillan Co., 1950.

Stender-Peterssen, A. "Russian Paganism," *Acta Jutlandica,* 28 (1956) pp 44–53.

Thomas, J. *Universal Pronouncing Dictionary of Biography and Mythology.* Philadelphia, Lippincott, 1950.

Vana, Z. *The World of the Ancient Slavs.* Detroit, Wayne State University Press, 1983, pp 83–103.

Vyncke, F. "The Religion of the Slavs." Bleeker, C. J. (ed.) *Historia Religionum.* Leiden. E. J. Brill, 1969–71. vol. 1, pp 649–66.

Zakharov, A. "The Statue of Zbrucz," *Eurasia septentrionalis antiqua,* 9 (1934) pp 336–48.

Zugta, Russell. "The Pagan Priests of Early Russia: Some New Insights," *Slavic Review.* 33 (1974) no. 2, pp 259–66.

Znayenko, M. *The Gods of the Ancient Slavs. Tatishchev and the Beginnings of Slavic Mythology.* Columbus, Slavica, 1980.

Znayenko, M. "Tatišcev's Treatment of Slavic Mythology." Ph.D. dissertation, Columbia University, 1973.

Forests of the Vampire: Slavic Myth. Time-Life Books, 1999.

SLAVIC PANTHEON

Divinities in the mythology and demonology of the Early Slavs

(Names used in this reconstruction include their versions in other systems of mythology, renderings and descriptions)

(Names used in this reconstruction include their versions in other systems of mythology, renderings and descriptions)

SUPERIOR DEITIES

A. FATHER OF THE GODS SVAROG—*the primeval, uncreated and eternal deity-demiurge, All-father, as well as the personification of the sustaining principle, his name being cognate with the Sanskrit* svar, *'bright clear or shining'; the artificer of the world who has withdrawn from outer activity*

B. SVAROZHICH (Svarogich)—*the supreme elemental god and* Svarog's *son, who was believed to preside over all the gods*

C. Other supreme native divinities—GODS
   PERUN (Pyerun)—*god of thunder and lightning, also of war and agriculture; his Norse and Teutonic counterpart is Thor(r), also known as Donar; Thursday is named after him while Wednesday comes from Odin's name (Thor's divine father), also spelt 'Woden'*
   RADEGAST (Radhost)—*a god of evening stars, fires and star light; presumably just an aspect of* Svantovit
   DAZHBOG—*a sky-deity, the god of light and fire, the giver of warmth,* Svarog's *son; believed to rule over the twelve kingdoms of the Zodiac, served by the two Auroras* (Zora, Zvezda)
   SVANTOVIT (Sventovit)—*the principal deity of the Slavonic Balts; god of gods; the god of husbandmen, prophesy and war; father of the Sun and fire; a white stallion, sacred to* Svantovit *and a means of divination, was kept in his chief temple at Arcona*

D. Other higher divinities—GODS
   VELES (Plentiful)—*the god of the underworld and harvest, also the patron god of farm cattle*
   STRIBOG (Striborg)—*the god of space, air and wind*
   ROD (One Who Promotes Birth)—*once a universal god, he was toppled from his position by* Perun *to be worshipped as a male deity of primeval fertility; protector of the home*
   SIM & RYGL—*twin deities, see* SIMARGL
   PROVE—*the god of justice and law*
   CHERNOBOG, the Black God (Chernoglav)—*a very unlikeable god of evil, darkness and death*
   BYELOBOG, the White God, or Byelun—*god of all things good, the personification of light and life (the opposite of* Chernobog*); usually portrayed as a venerable old man with a white beard*
   TRIGLAV (the Three-headed God)—*a god of war and husbandry*
   RUGIEVIT
   PORENUT (Porenutius) } *three divine brothers, gods of war and*
   POREVIT (Power)   *fertility*
   YAROVIT (He Who Welcomes Spring)—*a god of the spring revival; the embodiment of the spirit of vegetation and military strength*

YARILO (Summer-Bringer)—*initially a goddess of peace who changed gender and became the god of spring, fertility, harvest and erotic love; depicted as a barefoot youth in a white cloak and adorned with a crown of flowers*
PEREPLUT (One Who Endures)—*the god of memory*

E.   Other higher divinities—GODDESSES
CHORS—*a moon goddess, as well as the goddess of unrequited love, including lesbian*
PRIPELAGA—*the goddess of the earth and primeval fertility*
ZHIVA, SIVA (Alive)—*the goddess of summer and fruitfulness*
SIMARGL—*the bird goddess; a hybrid creature comprising the gods* SIM & RYGL, *a heavenly wet-nurse suckling divine babies, whom she feeds not on saliva but on the milk from her breasts*
MOKOSH (MOKOS)—*a goddess of sheep, weavers and fertility*
VESNA (Spring)—*the goddess of spring and young unbridled love*
MORENA, MARENA (Pestilence)—*the goddess of winter and death*
LADA (Beautiful)—*a goddess of spring, beauty and tender love*
PODAGA—*a female deity of weather*
PIZAMAR—*the goddess of music and art*

LESSER DIVINITIES
(Demons, Idols, Imaginary Beings)

A.   DEMONS of ELEMENTS *(of earth, water, air, fire and heavens)*
a.   Demons of Earth *(of the underworld, caves, mountains, rocks and stones)*
aa. Demons of the Underworld and Cavities
KOVLAD (Iron-keeper)—*the ruler over earth and cave treasures*
RUNA (Mistress of the Earth)—Kovlad's *wife*
PERMONIKS (Dwarfs)—*kobolds, supernatural creatures that were thought of as the guardians of mines and minerals*
LABUS (Ono Who Lures)—*a malignant spirit that lures children into caves*
ab. Demons of Mountains
MOUNTAIN VILE (pl., Fairies)—*nymphs dwelling in high, snow-capped, mountain ranges*
SVYATOGOR (the Giant of the Mountain)—*a huge mountain giant whose size exceeds even that of the highest mountains*
GIANTS ASHILKS—*spirits of ancestors who were believed to be a race of giants*
ac. Demons of Rocks and Stones
LAKTIBRADA, PIADIMUZHIK (Long Beard, Manikin)—*malicious mountain dwarf*
SPIRITS OF MAGICAL STONES—*invoked in divination and charms performed by means of stones and the rain water that gathers in rock holes and depressions*
b.   Water Demons (of the sea, rivers, lakes and ponds)
ba. Demons of the Sea
KING OF THE SEA, TSAR—*the lord of all sea creatures*
QUEEN OF THE SEA, TSARINA—*the wife of the King of the Sea*
SEA VILE/MAIDENS (pl., Rusalki, Mermaids)—*were believed to be the spirits of drowned lasses; they had an attractive and sexy human upper half with the tail of a fish instead of legs; they were believed to come ashore during the summer*
MONSTERS—*sea dragons and fabulous beasts*
bb. Demons of the Rivers
KING OF THE WATERS—*the lord of all the river spirits and creatures*
QUEEN OF THE WATERS—*the wife of the King of the Waters*
WATER VILE/NYMPHS—*diaphanous, golden-haired beauties of the water streams*
YUDAS (pl., Black Vile)—*evil nymphs who were believed to be responsible for drowning people*
DIVA (Divine Maiden)—*the chief of the* Rusalki, *or Mermaids; on moonlit nights they would assemble to dance and sing*
BEREHYNAS (pl., Who Dwell by the River-Side)—*evil nymphs who inhabit high river banks*
bc. Demons of the Lakes and Ponds
VODNIK (Vodyanoi, He Who Lives in Water)—*a local chief of the water demons and other divinities that inhabit any particular stretch of water; basically a good soul, he may at times be mischievous to the point of malevolence*

VODNICHKA (Water Mistress)—Vodnik's *wife; dwells in an underwater cave with her* *green husband who controls other water sprites and demons*

SAMODIVAS (Lonely Vile)—*water nymphs who dance alone at night*

c. Air Demons (of wind, air and weather)

ca. Wind Demons

OBLACHNIK (Cloud-giver)—*the Lord of the Winds and the Weather*

FROST (Grandfather Frost)—*a frost spirit; brother of* Oblachnik, *a good soul known* *for dispensing and delivering presents; in most Russian folk tales and legends,* *Frost appears as a nameless demon, often in the shape of a thin and hunched* *peasant man with gray hair and bushy white eyebrows; may be malevolent as* *well as benevolent*

POHVIZD (Whistler)—*a good-natured demon, the father of the winds who are loyal* *servants of the Lord of the Winds,* Oblachnik

VETERNITSA (Wind-bearer)—*the wife of* Pohvizd, *the mother of the five brother-winds*

VANOK (Breeze)—*the youngest of the winds*

VETRIK (Fan)—*the fourth of the brother-winds, a gentle, delightful wind*

VIKHOR (Whirlwind)—*the middle brother of the brother-winds; in Russian folklore a* *wicked enchanter personified as* Vikhor

SMRSHT (Tornado, Storm Wind)—*the second of the brother-winds*

HURRICANE—*the oldest of the five brothers, grim-faced and of gloomy disposition*

MELUZINA (Howling Wind)—*the youngest sister of the Winds believed to wail in the* *chimneys*

METELITSA (Snow-storm, Blizzard)—*the whimsical only daughter of Grandfather* *Frost, a malicious one, too, as she sends hails of snow*

CHMARNIK (He Who Brings Heavy Clouds)—*the ill-natured weather demon who* *gathers dark, rain-charged clouds to prevent the Sun from shedding its rays upon* *the earth; the author of much evil; the immortal evil agency; a fabulous creature* *with terrible talons; a devil*

cb. Air Demons/Demons of the Weather

YEZHIBABA, the Witch Baba Yaga—*an old crone, a malevolent witch and cannibal* *who flies on a broomstick and lives in the most remote and inaccessible part of a* *deep forest; in some Slavonic folk tales is the one in command of the Sun, Day and* *Night*

STRIGON, Wizard—*the brother of* Yezhibaba, *usually a malevolent divinity that can* *be propitiated and induced to behave benevolently; can alter his stature at pleasure*

CLOUD VILE/FAIRIES—*the daughters of* Oblachnik, *sylph-like and graceful, limpid* *and airy creatures*

FIERY DRAGONS—*the sons of* Yezhibaba (Baba Yaga), *vicious and malevolent, capable* *of transforming themselves into lightning and fiery balls; they abound in Russian* *legends and in popular belief are usually pictured with serpentine form or as various* *hybrid creatures*

d. Demons of the Fire

FIERY MAN—*a soul of an evil person appearing in the form of a fiery pole or a barrel;* *an agency inimical to people*

BLUDICHKI, WILL-O'-THE-WISP (pl., Ignes Fatui)—*souls of murdered women living over* *the marshes and graves as well as in rotten tree trunks; their deluding phosphorescent* *light is seen at night flitting about*

SVETLONOS, JACK-O'-LANTERN (Lantern-carrier)—*a sort of* ignis fatuus *in the corporeal* *form of a dwarf carrying a lantern on cold nights*

ZMOK, SPRITE—*a fiery little dragon or little snake, whirls along like a fiery ball, moving* *about amongst people in the form of a black chick*

RARACH, LITTLE RARACH (the Evil One, Imp)—*a fiery little falcon produced from the* *egg hatched under the stove*

PLEVNIK, HUSKIE (One Who Dwells Amidst the Husks)—*a demon who penetrates* *homes as he flies wildly in through a chimney in the form of a chain; similar to* Zmok, *appears in the form of a chick and enjoys sleeping in the husks*

e. Demons of the Heavenly Firmament

SUN—*the sun, male or female deity, a servant to or an attendant on the celestials, the* *supreme sky gods; gives brilliance and shine to the celebrated heavenly chariot;* Dazhbog *has been most often referred to as the earliest solar deity*

MOON—*Slavic* Mesiats *or* Myesyats, *the sister of the Sun and the moon deity who in* *the form of a bird drives* Chors, *a moon goddess, across the sky*

PLANETARIANS, PLANET SPIRITS—*the wandering souls of people who have been sacrificed; believed to be flitting to and fro; the guardian spirits of star lights*

ZORA, ZORYA, ZVEZDA, AURORA(S)—*the daughter and attendant of the Sun; in the evening called the Evening Star, or* Vetchertnitsa, *in the morning the Morning Star, or* Rannitsa *(in Russian mythology, Zvezda is actually a name given to its two guises,* Dennitsa *and* Zvezda Vetchernyaya, *the daughters of* Dazhbog)

RAINBOW—*the Sun's child by* Podaga; *despite the prominence of the sun deity in the Indo-European universe, the authorities still disagree on the gender of this ancient and shining divinity, conventionally associated with a radiant male god*

B. DEMONS of TIME

KING OF TIME—*incessantly dying and regenerating demon said to keep turning while seated on a mill stone*

TWELVE MONTHS (OR MOONS), FROM JANUARY THROUGH DECEMBER—*the sons of the King of Time*

KRACHUN (Shortie)—*the Master of the Winter Solstice; if a "badniak" (a tree trunk) had not been burnt to honor him, the displeased deity would make the days endless*

POLNOCHNITSA (Midnight Guest)—*a female divinity, whose appearance is believed to herald the impending death of family members*

POLUDNITSA (Midday Guest)—*a goddess of the fields; being a patron deity of farmers, she would punish those who worked in the fields at midday which she had decreed to be a time for taking a siesta; in Russian folklore, attended by* polovoi, *the spirit of the fields*

POLUDNICHEK (Midday Catcher in the Field)—*a pale little boy believed to have been chasing and punishing vermin during the midday siesta*

KL'AKANITSA (One Who Punishes)—*thought of as stealing and punishing children for lingering outside after the fall of night*

C. DEMONS of DESTINY:

SUDICHKI, THE THREE FATES (GOOD LUCK, MISERY, REVENGE)—*the daughters of the god* Prove, *goddesses who are regarded as the dispensers of fate to a new-born over its cradle*

DEATH—*an ominous divinity in the form of a white skeleton carrying a scythe, who was thought of as accompanying the dead on their way to the underworld*

KMINSKA KMOTRA, THE THIEVING GOD MOTHER—*a gossipmonger, popularly believed to take the property of all those who had dared to challenge their decreed lot*

D. WOODLAND/SYLVAN DEMONS:

LESOVIK, SYLVANUS (Woodie, Sylvan Dwarf, the Lord of the Woods, the Wild Man, Div, Nickola)—*a demon-god, one of the widespread class of wood-spirits that were believed to live in the forest; a* ljeshii *(from the Russian 'ljes' meaning 'wood'); represented as an old little man in appearance, his body covered all over with tangled hair; a woodland deity with sprouting horns, sharing many characteristics with the Satyrs, Pan and the Italian Fauns; can alter his stature at pleasure; sitting in a tree, he would set riddles, by way of penalty, for noisy human visitors of the forest*

WOODLAND VILE (pl., Sylvan Fairies/Nymphs)—*graceful dryads dwelling in oaks and linden trees*

GRGALITSA (She Who Belches)—*an evil sylvan nymph believed to tease and tantalize careless men*

MAMUNA—*a sylvan spirit, a voluptuous nymph with very large breasts*

PREMIEN, SHAPE-SHIFTER—*one of the body of sylvan demons; woodland phantom that would scare people out of their wits by night*

BORUTA (Bark-skinned)—*a woodland spirit of nature dwelling in the ruins scattered all over the High Tatra Mountains, Slovakia's major mountain range and reference point of the national identity of the Slovaks*

E. DEMONS of the FIELDS

RYE OLD FATHER (Polevik, the Master of the Field, Polovoi, a Field-spirit)—*a field elf/spirit/brownie who dominates all the creatures living in the fields (both spirits and animals); protean by nature, he can turn into a three-head creature with fiery tongues*

RYE OLD WOMAN, RYE BABA—*the wife of the Rye Old Man with a liking for scaring people, known to favor peas as her staple food*

133

Rye Maiden—*belongs in the company of field vile; or fairies, and is depicted as carrying a sickle and a whetstone*

Belon (the Whitish One)—*the father of* Poludnichek, *a field-spirit who helps out in reaping grains during harvest time*

Sporish, Thriftie—*a spirit that Rye Old Father uses to chase away the thieves and make sure that the fields do not catch fire (from Rye Old Father's fire-spitting tongues)*

F. DOMESTIC DEMONS *(elves, brownies, domovois, and other goblins that like to play tricks on people and vex them)*

a. Household Brownies—assistants

Gazdichko (Little Household Manager), Domovik, Domovoi—*the spirit of a family's founding ancestor; a brownie that helps the family and looks after its welfare*

Hadovik (Little Snake)—*a helpful domestic spirit very much like* Gazdichko; *was believed to dwell under the threshold*

Lasica, Weasel—*nimble helping spirit*

Chlevnik, Cattle-Shed Hand—*the stinking spirit of sheds and stables; if fed by a good master of the house, he would help around the barn*

Humnik, Threshing-Floor Hand—*a brownie with straw hair who helps around the threshing-floor*

Vintsurik, Wine-Sampler (Cellar Man, Vineyard Crone)—*a spirit that helps perform chores about wine cellars; represented with a reddish nose and known to keep singing, otherwise hiccups*

Pikulik, Sweet-Toothie—*a goblin that helps wagon men; known to enjoy best being carried along in a wagon man's overcoat side-pocket, where he nibbles on crumbs*

b. Other Domestic Spirits

Kikimora—*a female domestic spirit, an ugly nuisance that harms the male animals, prevents other domestic brownie-helpers from performing household chores for busy housekeepers and makes yarn get tangled; wakes the children at night by tickling them*

Betiah, Madra (Rogue, Cheat-monger)—*a wicked wood-goblin reputed to goad people into cheating and forgery*

Korgorusha—*a female domestic spirit in rivalry with* Kikimora; *was said to live at home in the guise of a cat and to steal things and drag them home, which would cause friction between people*

Basilisk—*a modern monster and an imaginary successor of the* Gorgons *and* Chymeras *and superstitions associated with these; it used to enjoy an existence in the popular belief in different forms, particularly as the king of the serpents*

G. HUMAN-SHAPE DEMONS:

Matoha, Babiak (Phantom, Ghost, Specter)—*an apparition known and dreaded for the ability to change form into shades, whitish figures, and to make mysterious noises; would turn up on the sites of accidents and misfortunes, but equally everywhere where some sort of treasure might have been hidden; the places most frequented by this phantom include fortresses, castles, mills, crossroads and cemeteries*

Mora (Nightmare)—*a scary phantom believed to possess the souls of dead relatives or of living people deep in sleep; the legend surrounding Nightmare says that this phantom may even strangle people while they are asleep*

Upir (Vampire)—*a demon entering the bodies of people who have been buried alive; a corpse that would come back to life at night to suck the blood of the living (both human and animal) to sustain its tragic existence; the name itself is a borrowing from the Serbian 'vampir'*

Vlkodlak (Werewolf)—*a demon inhabiting a person who has drunk from a wolf's footprint, possibly a vampire who had changed form into the wolf (at times metamorphosed into a bat); some werewolves are believed to have the ability to assume different guises involuntarily under the influence of the moonlight, but sometimes, legend says, they metamorphose at pleasure*

Ivan Hudec
with Emma Nezinska

Slovak Books

from
Bolchazy-Carducci Publishers, Inc.

Images Gone with Time
Photographic Reflections of Slovak Folk Life
ISBN: 0-86516-436-3, Hardbound

Slovenčina pre cudzincov
Hardbound, ISBN 0-86516-446-0; Workbook: Paperback, ISBN 0-86516-447-9
Set of 3 Cassettes: Audiocassettes, ISBN 0-86516-448-7
Complete Package: ISBN 0-86516-449-5

Slovak for You
Paperback, ISBN 0-86516-331-6; Set of 2 Cassettes, ISBN 0-86516-469-X

English-Slovak Dictionary
Hardbound, ISBN 0-86516-226-3

English/ Slovak-Slovak/English Dictionary
Hardbound, ISBN 0-86516-443-6

Slovakia: The Heart of Europe
Hardbound, ISBN 0-86516-319-7

Slovensko moje
Hardbound, ISBN 0-86516-318-9

A Slovak History:
A Struggle for Sovereignty in Central Europe
Forthcoming, Paperback, ISBN 0-86516-426-6
Hardbound, ISBN 0-86516-500-9

Trapped in the Old Mine
ISBN 0-86516-466-5

Zuska of the Burning Hills
ISBN 0-86516-467-3

Misko
ISBN 0-86516-465-7

Eight Centuries of the Slovak Heraldry
Hardbound, ISBN: 0-86516-458-4

Slovak History:
Chronology and Lexicon
Forthcoming, Paperback, ISBN 0-86516-444-2
Hardbound, ISBN 0-86516-500-9

Lexikón slovenských dejín
Hardbound, ISBN 0-86516-445-2

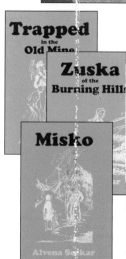

Bolchazy-Carducci Publishers, Inc.

1000 Brown Street, Unit 101, Wauconda, IL 60084 USA
Phone: 847/526-4344; *Fax:* 847/526-2867
www.bolchazy.com

Drawing of a reconstruction of a sacral cult site of the god Perun from the tenth century, near Novgorod at the mouth of the Volchova River at Lake Ilmen in Russia. This place is characterized by three circular ditches with wooden idols in the center. It was found in the area of the monastery in Peryn. Long after the original site was destroyed by the local monks, sailors sailing by used to throw coins as a sacrifice into the waters of Volchova River.